Shift

Lindsey Madison

Published by Madison Dunn, 2012.

Shift

By Lindsey Madison
Copyright 2013 Lindsey Madison
Smashwords Edition

While every precaution has been taken in the preparation of this book, the publisher assumes no responsibility for errors or omissions, or for damages resulting from the use of the information contained herein.

SHIFT

First edition. December 31, 2012.

ISBN: 979-8224435913

Written by Lindsey Madison.

Chapter 1

I walk quickly over stones covered in dried leaves, as my face collides with cold, morning air. Cloudy mist spills out over waves of lavender in a clearing below. I slow down as out of the corner of my eye, I see two figures moving. They are foxes. Their tails like flames, they prance around each other, and play catch-me-if-you-can in the soft morning light. It happens before I can stop them, before I can even call-out, my heart sinks as I watch the smaller one playfully jump back, pressing her leg into a metal trap. The sharp metal teeth clutch her leg and she cries out in agony. Her partner desperately circles her, howling in despair.

The beeping alarm jerks me out of the meadow and back into reality. It is 6:05, and I have forty-five minutes to pull it together for my first day at a brand new school. As I brush my teeth I ponder how this had happened. My father, got to love him, had decided it would be "better for everyone involved" if I packed up my things and moved six hundred miles to Colorado to live with my mom. He said he was "just too busy with work, and that I needed someone there at night." Maybe he was right. Maybe I was getting lonely, but I didn't like the idea of starting all over with a whole new group of strangers in the middle of my junior year.

As I examine the sky-blue color of my irises, and pretend it is the first time I've ever seen them, I whisper, "Hi, Amy." I smile sympathetically at myself in the mirror and try to make it look real.

Downstairs I pour myself a tall glass of organic coconut milk. Skye Goldin, my homeopathic doctor, says I have a "highly sensitive and erratic allergic disorder" and so I eat mostly nuts and berries. The few times I have tried to eat french fries, or anything fried, my tongue protrudes out of my mouth like a giant slug from the allergic reaction.

"Don't forget your vitamins!" My mom shouts down the hall.

The truth is I couldn't forget my vitamins if I tried. The plastic container is on the counter and there is another one in my lunch bag.

You could say mother is overcompensating for not taking care of me the past two years, but the truth is she has always been like this.

"And don't forget tennis today after school!" she bellows.

Tennis. Did I mention my mother loves tennis? She plays in three tennis leagues and got a scholarship for it in college. I am more like the "I'll try not to trip over and die" sort of player. There's a reason I have really expensive health insurance.

"Are you sure that tennis is necessary?"

"Yes. Totally necessary. You will meet lots of new friends at tennis!" she sings.

Her high heels click onto the kitchen floor. My mom really is stunning. Although, I prefer her without all of the makeup and nylon.

"Okay ... sure. I'll see you after school," I manage.

"Not without a hug!" she says.

After having all of the air squeezed out of my lungs, and several enormous lipstick kisses on my cheek (my mom's lips vaguely resemble a sucker-fish), I'm on my way to school.

The crowd here is intense. It looks like a page from "Where's Waldo" except with more cleavage and swearing. No one seems to notice me, but that doesn't stop the pounding of my heart as I play frogger with the crowd and make my way to room 306.

The room is empty except for the teacher sitting at a large desk staring at a computer screen. I drop my bag onto a desk, and she looks up from her trance.

"Mrs. Hennessey?" I ask hesitantly.

"You must be new." She sighs and reaches mechanically for the cup of coffee on her desk.

"Yea. I just moved. I'm Amy..." She just stares at me so I continue, "Amy Kitcher."

"Kitcher. That name isn't on my roster yet. You will have to check it out with the counselors later. We are writing research essays so you will want to find something you are interested in..."

A line of kids fills the room and the yelling and teasing drowns out her voice.

"Don't be a douche!" A girl cries out in exasperation as a boy pinches her arm.

Everyone has someone to talk to except me. I begin to draw curvy lines on my notebook and try to blend in. Finally, the bell rings and Mrs. Hennessey gets everyone's attention, points in my direction and announces,

"There's a new student in class, her name is Amy Kitcher."

I lift my hand to say hi as if I'm being sworn into testify at court, as all eyes turn to stare at me. My stomach does a couple of serious turns. Some of the quieter kids actually smile. A few really pretty girls with extra makeup raise their eyebrows and contort their faces.

Jealousy is a tricky thing. I want to tell them I'm not going to steal your guy, I'm not even sure I like guys. But it's too late. I've been identified as "the new girl" and this phrase, this label, will inevitably attract male attention. Several from the football clan are already starting to fall over each other, trying to show off.

"Dude, can't wait to kick some ass at the game tonight." A taller boy in a red jersey elbows another boy glancing back in my direction.

"Jeremy, pull it together. Let's focus. We have a lot of things to accomplish today," Mrs. Hennessey orders the room.

I sit back and breathe a sigh of relief. Just as my blood pressure is returning to something normal, a tall boy with dirty blonde hair struts into the room and looks directly at me. Stunned, I glimpse the corner of his lips curving up to smile before I turn away. His green eyes are mischievous. He looks like a real life version of Peter Pan. He hands Mrs. Hennessey a pass and sits down two desks in front of me.

"Patrick Flynn, you always have a pass!" Mrs. Hennessey laughs.

"I know you like them," he grins.

Mrs. Hennessey laughs and swats at him playfully. "You are too much."

Who was this guy? Who gets away with that? Come in late and schmooze the teacher? I can't focus on the assignment and find myself staring half-angry, half-curious, at different parts of him during class. Something about the way he moves, he is so comfortable; every part of him looks effortless. His hand falls loosely off the desk and reaches into his bag to take out his notebook. I drift in and out of focus between expository sentences and the composition of muscle and bone sitting two desks in front of me.

The bell rings and I follow him out the door into the hall where we are swept up in the traffic of the hall. If you didn't know any better you would think it was some kind of emergency evacuation. He high-fives three different people as he passes easily through the crowd. I lose track of him somewhere in the 600 hall and make my way to gym class. I almost forget about him until tennis practice.

Coach Clement has everyone warm up doing rounds of stretches.

"Okay! Side stretch! Reach those arms! Don't let me catch you slacking!"

He is wearing a purple spandex shirt that is a size too small and his shorts look like a keepsake from the 70's. His voice is loud and scratchy probably from smoking and if it weren't for his clothes, you would think he was a military commander. After the round of stretches he lines us up. I nervously grasp my racket and wonder if anyone would notice if I very slowly ran far away.

"Since the girls have been beating the pants off everyone they play, today we are going to mix it up," Clement barks, "Girls against the boys. Let's see if these ladies can teach you boys how it is done."

I want to pop like a zit. Does he even realize what he is saying? I don't really know how to play tennis. I really have no business being on the team. The next thing I know, I'm standing across the tennis court, ready to serve a ball to Patrick Flynn.

His blond hair flopping like a sail in the wind, Patrick is doing warm-ups on the court. Jumping up and down he jokes, "I don't know if

I can handle this. Go easy on me… I'm just a boy!" He takes some long breaths in and out and does a side-angle stretch trying to act serious in his preparation.

"Just so you know, I'm not that good at this," I say. "That was a preemptive apology."

"A what?"

"A pre-emp-tive ap-o-lo-gy!" I retort.

"Does that mean you have a disease or something?" he says. "Thanks for the warning."

"You're welcome!" I shout, and serve the ball.

The ball lands out of bounds and after a second try it is his serve. The ball comes flying across the net directly in range and I manage to volley it back over. He misses the shot, and it is my serve. The sun radiates like a gigantic furnace in the sky, and the sweat runs down my back. Patrick's confidence also radiates as he crouches, knees bent, bobbing like a tiger.

"Why don't you service me lassie!" he calls out in a fake Irish accent. "I haven't got all day you know!" he taunts.

I glare across the net. I actually want to hit him hard with the ball, if only to get him to shut up for a few minutes. I contemplate the likelihood of this actually happening as I swing my racket to hit the ball across the court. The ball flies up in the air and I watch it closely, seeing the tiny lime-green hairs turning through the air as it connects with my racket. Time seems slower and my arm moves with super speed through the air whacking the ball with a clear "ping" and sending it slicing across the net and curving toward Patrick's face.

He glares in disbelief as he rubs his jaw. "Sweet juicy crepes! That really hurt!"

"You, know what? I'm a little bit sorry!" I say laughing.

"Just a little bit?"

"Yea." I motion with my fingers squeezed almost together, "Just this much."

"Alright, that's it. You asked for it." He shakes his head as he tosses the ball to the ground at his feet. It bounces quickly back into his hand. "I have no choice now, but to kick your little hinny."

"Bring it" I demand forgetting to second-guess myself.

He serves the ball again. I focus my attention to see the word "Penn" turning through the air. My legs seem to move without even trying and I slam the ball across the court. I turn to look, proud of my accomplishment, and realize I am all the way on the adjacent court. A girl with long red hair lowers her racket and stares at me. Even Patrick looks stunned. He just stands there speechless. I turn to see the coach and the other players. Everyone looks confused and motionless. Looks of fear and awe surface on their faces.

"How did you do that?" Patrick asks. "How did you hit that ball?"

"I ... I guess I don't know." My mind is reeling as I try to catch my breath.

Coach Clement walks across the court. "That was amazing! I've never seen anything like it, but it was just amazing." He looks dumbfounded.

I try to shrug it off, but Patrick looks at me and then at the ground, as if he recognizes something.

After practice, I work through some geometry problems and help mom with dinner, spaghetti squash and pine nuts. She asks me about my day, and fortunately when I tell her it went fine, she moves on to other subjects so I can pretend nothing unusual happened. It's not until bedtime that I lay awake thinking about the tennis match. Had I done something amazing? Maybe it was some kind of fluke like when a comet comes too close it messes with gravity and space and time. Or maybe I was like the hulk. Maybe when I get angry I am able to move at lightning speed and whack moving objects. I'm not saying I need anger management classes, but I have been upset before, lots of times, and nothing like this has ever happened. I remember the look on Patrick's face. He acted as if he knew something, as if he'd seen it before. After a little tossing and turning, I finally drift off to sleep and dream of the hulk playing tennis with comets.

Chapter 2

The alarm rings as I roll out of my dream about racket ball and giant squid. Out of the shower my hair resembles the tentacles of the squid monster, long dark strands roll across my back. I towel dry those little squid arms as I look squarely in the mirror and give myself a pep-talk.

"Okay, self. I know this is only your second day of school, but you've got to make some friends. I know you are OCD and I know your hands shake when you are nervous, but that is no excuse. You are just going to have to grow a pair and make some friends."

As I contemplate the numerous psychological issues of a female chiding herself to grow male reproductive organs, my mother comes into my room.

"Amy Hale Kitcher, what is this mess?" my mother thunders.

"Mess, this is my mom. Mom this is my mess." I answer sarcastically.

"You know I like to keep a clean house," she orders.

"I know mom." I answer obediently. "I'll clean it up before school."

Sometimes I feel this little part of me shriveling inside when I say whatever someone wants, as if it is physically recoiling from the exchange. The good news is when I do, the other person usually leaves me alone.

At school, everyone is excited because next week is "Spring Break." Kids buzz around the cafeteria like bees drunk on sprite with their fingers pressed to their phones hovering over each other as if the possibility of pills were pollen waiting in each other's pockets.

I watch as Coach Clement comes bounding down the hall, "Amelia! I can't wait to see what you do in practice after the break!" His scratchy voice echoes down the hall. "We'll be going to state for sure," he adds with a dramatic thumbs-up.

"It's Amy," I start, but he is halfway down the hall before I can explain. I make my way to Physics down by the rooms that smell of chloroform.

It is only halfway through the hour, and my pencil strolls up and around the page, like a lost traveler asking for directions, slowly marking the outline of a human face. Mrs. Watercross is bellowing out the climax of her lesson, and I focus my vision on the eyes in my drawing. Something about the eyes seems alive, as if I have felt their gaze before. This is just a drawing, I try to comfort myself, but the glints of flame in the center send shivers down my back.

Mrs. Watercross's diatribe drifts back, "Time travel could be possible, if particles have the ability to move faster than the speed of light. Energy has shifted into matter and matter could shift into energy..."

Was it possible that the weird thing at tennis practice yesterday could just be time travel? Did that mean that I was making particles move faster than the speed of light? Slowing down time? I almost drop my pencil at the thought of me being faster than light. Who was I kidding? I was the one who had to drop out of tap-lessons due to the massive bruises from so much falling. I remember the look on Patrick's face after I hit him with the ball. I wonder where he is, and find myself reminiscing on the arch of his hand in English class.

After lunch I am back in class with Mr. Flynn himself and I hide my shaky palms under the desk. He once again struts into the class late.

"I know I only have two chances left," he says assuredly, handing our teacher a pass.

"Mr. Flynn, your luck will run out if you're not careful." Mr. Keller is the tallest man I've ever seen. His bald head shines in the fluorescent light and his voice bounds across the room as Patrick takes a seat in the row next to me.

"Nice moves yesterday," he whispers across the row.

"Where do you get all of these passes?" I ask. The words ring in complete silence. Somehow I missed the cue to shut up. I look over and see Mr. Keller turning toward me.

"We have a new student in class today." He points his yardstick at me. I'm definitely being singled out for speaking out of turn. "Ms. Kitcher, say hello."

I manage a small wave to the class. "Hello" I say, turning a deeper shade of embarrassment.

Mr. Keller starts off on a lecture on "Mill," going on about the tyranny of the majority while the rest of the class settles into a half drool, or sneaks video footage on their i-pods. They only wake up when they hear "pop quiz". Staring at the list of 100 questions, I get the "pop" part, but wonder what part of Mr. Keller thought this was a "quiz." When we are finished, we trade with a partner to grade them. Patrick hands me his "quiz."

I don't look at it at first. Mr. Keller seems intent on making sure my corner of the room is paying attention. It isn't until we start grading them that I see a hand-scribbled message on the bottom.

We should talk tonight. 667-8950

I stare at the message with a puzzled expression. Seriously, where does he get off? Does he really think he is all that? I could turn it in this way, but I already have developed a reputation in this class, history – my favorite subject of all places. I copy his phone number down and slip it into my pocket. Then I carefully erase the message and finish grading his answers. I don't believe the results: he got every single answer right. I check with a couple of students to make sure I didn't miss something, and the highest grade anyone else got is a 66%. He must have cheated. He's a pass stealing cheater, but a really darn cute one. As the bell rings I get up to leave and feel Patrick watch me go, waiting no doubt for some kind of response to his note. When I finally turn to look he is gone.

My mom and I have a thing for Italian food. Since I'm allergic to most processed food, we make our own pasta. Mom is mixing the dough when I get home from school.

"How was your day?" she asks

"Fine if you don't count failing a history 'quiz.'"

"But I thought history was your best subject?"

"Not this week." I shrug.

She hands me the spoon to help shift the dough into the pasta maker.

"Your tennis coach called and he said you were awesome yesterday. He wants to give you private lessons over the break," she says enthusiastically

"I'd rather not." I say pulling out the lettuce. I sink my hand into the plastic bag, running cold water over the fragile green leaves. "I was thinking about taking a little break from tennis," I say looking up at her hopefully.

"Absolutely not." Her weight shifts back, and I know she is serious. "How many times have you quit something?" She demands. "Swimming, karate, ballet, gymnastics, tai-chi, piano... I can't believe you quit piano."

"Tennis is your thing, mom, I want to do my thing," I plead.

"Why can't you just trust me? I have done this all before, and I don't want you to end up making the wrong choices." She slams the spoon onto the counter.

"Why can't I make any choices? Is my life just a second chance for you? So I'm going to just skip my own life until it matches what you want." I reach for a towel on the counter and swing it hard onto into the sink. "Okay! Let's send my life down the drain." I strain to catch my breath. "How about I just sleep through college and wake up an engineer working on alternative energy. Does that sound good?"

"Don't be so selfish."

I can feel hot burning tears cover my face as I contemplate those words. Selfish? Was it selfish to want to make your own choices? Even if they are mistakes.

"It's like you brought me to an amusement park with all these great rides and you want me to just watch or repeat the ones you liked. Do you want me to just skip my own ride?"

The words are so mangled by frustrated rage, if my mom heard them, she definitely didn't comprehend them. I run out of the kitchen, grab my bag and cry, "I'm going for a walk," as I slam the door behind me.

I wipe the tears from my face and contemplate the burning in my throat. Why is it when I get really mad, everything comes streaming out in a river of really bad metaphors? I march steadily down the sidewalk. I really have no idea where I am going, but every step feels a little better. I wonder through the neighborhood, across a wide stretch of grass and end up staring at a giant sculpture of a polar bear. The stone is pure white and the hollowed out eyes stare straight ahead. I move closer to the stream below and find a ten foot sculpture of a dragonfly perched above the moving water, and for a second it almost seems real. I remember when I was little, and I had to leave my mom to visit my dad, I embroidered a dragonfly on a piece of cloth for my mom with the words, "I will always fly home to you." I can't help but tear up thinking about this now. I remember the note from Patrick's test, and pull out his number from by back pocket. As I dial the number a tingling sensation comes back into my fingers and I feel a warm hum in my stomach. He answers after the first ring.

"Amy Kitcher. I was hoping you would call."

"How did you know it was me?" I say.

"I just knew. Where are you? Can I meet you somewhere?"

"I'm sitting next to a giant dragonfly that looks like it could eat me for dinner," I laugh.

"Oh, yeah? That sounds pretty dangerous. You are in the sculpture park. I'll be there in ten minutes."

"Okay," I sigh.

After we hang up I take my shoes off and wade into the stream. The temperature is freezing but it feels good to be a part of the moving water. I let it wash over my calves and pretend I am the first human to ever touch the rolling stones beneath my feet. Just when I stop expecting him, Patrick's voice calls from above,

"I found you," he says, and jumps down onto a boulder in the middle of the stream. I wade back onto the ground and put my hands on the back of my hips.

"You wanted to talk?" I ask.

"Yea. Can we walk for a bit?" he asks

As I put my shoes on, Patrick wraps his arms around the giant sycamore tree next to the stream. "Aren't these fantastic? Sometimes I swear you can hear them talk," he says looking at me and smiling.

"Really." I say sarcastically

"Yes, this one says you are being skeptical only on the surface, and the truth is you talk to trees all the time."

I smile as we make our way onto a path trailing down toward a kid's play area and swing set.

"So, do you wanna tell me how you managed to hit a tennis ball going ninety miles an hour from a completely different court?"

"I really don't know how I did that. I think it must have been some kind of a space-time warp from a passing comet ... or maybe I'm the hulk," I say trying to smile. The embarrassment of this moment surprises me. I feel kind of freakish, like the bearded woman at the circus, and change the subject. "How did you get every single answer right on Keller's test? Why are you so ... lucky?" I pull myself onto the swing and stretch my heels out into the sand gently swinging forward.

"You think I cheated," he says smiling. "The truth is I can feel which answer Keller thinks is right. It's just a feeling. The right answers have a different feel to them."

"Really."

I look up at him as the sun's light turns to dusk and a soft haze envelops the air. His green eyes almost glow in the light.

"I know this is going to sound crazy, but it's not just luck. I am a coder," he confesses.

"A coder?"

"Someone who is able to create events by directing their thoughts. I think you're one too."

I get up from the swing and strain to look in his eyes. For the first time since I met him they are serious, and completely clear. I just stand there looking at him trying to figure out if he is certifiably crazy.

"You don't believe me," he says. "But you will."

"Are you saying you can jump off of buildings and not die?" I challenge.

"Maybe." He grins. "I haven't tried that one before, but it sounds fun."

"And you think because I ran across two tennis courts I am one of these 'coder people'?" I respond crossing my arms.

"Yea, I think so," he says. "Technically everyone is, but most people can't focus their thoughts that well. I know some people who have spent their whole lives trying to do what you did yesterday."

"Run really fast?" I ask.

"Slow down time," he says crossing his arms. We look like two samurai masters, facing off with our arms crossed.

"How could I slow down time? Wouldn't I have to move faster than the speed of light? That's impossible..."

His hands make their way to my shoulders, and I feel the weight of his arms resting casually across my collarbone. "Come with me for one week. If you want answers, I know where to find them. You have to meet someone."

"Come with you where?" I ask trying to maintain a shred of composure while standing under his arms, staring into his eyes, by a lake, at sunset. It's like we are on the cover of some cheesy romance novel.

"Just one week. It's spring break. You won't even have to miss school."

"I can't just leave," I protest repressing images of Gone with the Wind.

He smiles, leans forward and in one sweeping motion he is walking upside down on his hands. His shirt slips down to unveil several budding ripples of abdomen muscle, and I have to remind myself that I'm not the kind of girl who falls for that kind of stuff.

"Yes, you can," he says walking his hands across the grass. "I have a new contraption, it is called a car. Have you heard of it?" He collapses onto his feet and turns to go. "Meet me at my house at 7:30 tomorrow morning. You don't have to trust me. Listen to your heart – it will tell you what to do. Just don't think too much about it!"

I watch him disappear over the hill. I am starting to feel like maybe this is the circus, but at least I'm not the only freak.

Chapter 3

"I know it sounds crazy, but I really feel I can trust him." I plead.

"Let me get this straight. You are going to a destination unknown, on a road trip to meet someone you don't know, with a guy you just met?" My best friend, Ally, is making some good points.

"Look, I don't know what it is, but I feel different around him. It's like I'm changing inside and I need to know what is going on." I say stretching my back and nestling myself in the heaping pile of pillows on my bed.

"This sounds like you are falling pretty hard for this guy. Did you see Romeo and Juliet? It doesn't end well Amy. And now you want me to lie to your mother so you can run off and end up with a tag on your toe? I don't think so."

"I'm not falling for him!" I counter sitting back up. "All I need is for you to cover for me if my mom calls to check in. Let her think I am visiting you this week. Come on Ally, I need your help. You are my best friend. Please!" I pulled the best friend card. She can't possibly say no, right? There is a long pause on the other line, as I hold my breath waiting for her reply. "Ally?" I ask carefully as if her silence were a dark room.

"Okay. I'll do it," she finally says. "But you are going to text me every day, and the second you don't, I'm calling the authorities, and telling your mother."

"Okay, fair enough. Look, I really appreciate this."

"And you are going to visit me for real first chance you get this summer," she adds.

"I'll be there for real I promise." I say goodbye telling her how great she is repeatedly until she gets sick of it and hangs up. Yawning and nearly asleep, my fingers scroll down one more time to the previous messages and I smile to see Patrick's text.

GAS 1632 West Plum Street. That is where I live. CYT – DBL

The next morning as I look at all of the stuffed animals, my hula hoop, and the countless pictures of me growing up, I realize the full extent of the crazy thing I am about do. If I were in Ally's position I wouldn't let her do this. So what makes me think going on a road trip someplace unknown is a good idea? I remember Patrick's green eyes and my pulse quickens. He was right. My heart is telling me to go, and if I keep thinking, I'll talk myself out of it. I take the cash stashed from my birthday and throw my favorite jeans, a hair brush, my phone, some clean underwear and my coziest sweatshirt into a bag. I almost leave without my toothbrush and my Pink Floyd t-shirt. I look in the mirror for a quick pep talk.

"Okay. You are maybe crazy, but you are on a mission to uncover great mysteries of the universe, and to be back before your mom finds out. Don't blow it." I smile at the fact that I can crack myself up, and look one last time to see a hint of fear reveal itself in my eyes.

Downstairs my mom is reading a magazine on the couch. She thinks I am driving up to see Ally, and this is the hard part: straight up, face to face, lying to my mom.

"Hey, mom." I start.

"Hey sweetie."

"I'm really sorry for fighting last night," I say.

"It's okay honey. I wish you weren't leaving for the break. We could use the bonding time you know?" She's right. We could use some bonding time. I pull on a piece of my t-shirt, winding it into a knot and cutting off the circulation to my finger.

"I know. But Ally really needs me right now. Kyle broke up with her," I lie. "And it will be good for me too." I avert my eyes, and try not to think about anything.

"Come here honey," she says, reaching her arms around me. "I just want you to be happy."

A tear of guilt streams down my face as I hug her. I wipe it off on her shoulder.

"I filled your vitamin containers with extra B to help you drive." She smiles, scrunching my face and giving me a huge kiss on my forehead. "Be safe."

"I'll be back on Sunday." I say waving goodbye and closing the door behind me.

I let out a huge sigh of relief as I roll the car out of the driveway and head down the street to find Patrick's house. The road is empty except for a few bleary eyed joggers and I feel the hum of my engine vibrating into the steering wheel as I pass by a large brassy sign announcing "Essex Park." I pull my Honda Civic a.k.a "the Fugitive," into the driveway of what looks like a nineteenth century mansion. There is a four car garage and giant sculpted lions at the entrance. The doorway is surrounded by stained glass irises. I ring the bell.

"I'll be down in a second." Patrick's voice comes out of the speaker on the wall.

He comes out the door with three wolf-looking dogs bounding around him. "Settle down guys, I'll take you with me next time I promise." He turns his inescapable grin up toward me. "You made it. I was beginning to think you weren't coming."

The steady look in his eyes catches me off guard, and somehow I can't look directly at him.

"Don't you want to shave or something? You look pretty scruffy." I say pushing one of the giant slobber-machines off my shoulder.

"Scruffy?" he asks rubbing the five o'clock shadow on his jaw.

"I'll drive," I add.

"No, let me drive. I love driving and I know all the short cuts," he insists, pushing the garage door code.

The door lifts up, revealing a shiny black car with the BMW logo on the hood. I roll my eyes.

"A BMW? Really? Is this necessary?" I ask. I really am a snob when it comes to wealthy people.

"What? This old thing?" He smiles throwing our bags in the back seat.

"You could drive my car," I offer.

"Oooh. I've always wanted to travel in a candy wrapper on wheels," he replies sarcastically. "Maybe next time."

"I'll have you know that car is a total trooper. This is the Fugitive, and she has gotten me through some super tight spots, sporting way more awesomeness than whatever you call your night-rider over there."

"Okay, I'm sorry," he says turning to face me. "Let's put "the Fugitive" in the garage where he will be safe."

"She. Where she will be safe," I correct him.

"Where she will be safe," he amends. I step to the left to move my car. He steps to the right and our hips brush slightly. I can feel his breath fall near my ear. The blood pumps from my heart like a thoroughbred racing directly to my cheeks.

"Sorry," I say looking away.

"Don't be," he says, flashing a quick embarrassed smile. While I move "the Fuge", he pulls the BMW out of the driveway. I see my reflection in the shiny black door which easily clicks open without a sound. I pause for a second before getting in.

"What are you waiting for?" he asks.

I take a deep breath and make an effort to collect myself. I wonder if extra vitamin B calms raging hormonal reactions. Looking up, I see a flock of birds fly in a V-shape, headed south. The clouds are moving so fast I can almost feel the Earth moving. Somehow I take this to be a good omen as I step into the tan leather seat and within minutes we are headed down the street to a destination unknown.

I roll down the window with the all too silent push of a button, and try to acclimate to the new car smell. I angle my hips down, stretch out the kink in my back and let a few strands of my hair out of the window to play in the current. Patrick looks at home shifting the gear down, and I notice the green of his eyes light up as he looks over and smiles at me.

"So where are we going?" I ask as we make a sharp turn onto the highway.

"New Mexico," he answers. "I want you to meet someone."

For a guy whose mouth spends most of its time half-open in some kind of smile, Patrick strangely resembles a vault. How can a person divulge so little and expect so much? Trying to repress the feeling that I am going to be the kid on the milk carton, I restrain myself and ask politely,

"Who do you want me to meet?"

"It's actually a group of people," he offers.

"A group of 'coders'?" I poke.

"You could say that."

We turn off the highway and into a gas station. While Patrick runs the gas pump I run into the Circle K to stock up on snacks. I come out bearing Cracker Jacks, nuts, and bottled water.

"Cracker Jacks! I love Cracker Jacks," he says desperately.

I'm a little surprised to see his eyes widen with anticipation, and wonder if there is some kind of secret additive lacing the caramel that I don't know about. "I'm not sure you can handle the Jacks quite yet," I say wryly, stashing the box in the glove compartment as we pull back onto the highway.

We drive for a few miles in silence. I study Patrick's profile while he focuses on the road. I notice the mischief in his eyes is accentuated by a darker brow line that jets upward making it look like he is always raising an eye-brow. His jaw is flecked with stubble, and his face is striking yet soft somehow. He smiles, having caught me staring, and I quickly resume looking out the window.

There is a rhythm to the ride, and I start to notice the tiny details in the wood on the telephone polls as the fibers push behind us like pages turning. A warm glow rises in my stomach. For a second everything slows down, and I can see the grass in the prairie bend like a bowstring drawing back. A grasshopper catapults off a blade and we seem to be going less than five miles an hour, which is impossible on a highway. I come out of this trance and notice Patrick staring at me.

"What?" I say.

"You really are beautiful," he says.

"Right," I say sarcastically. "And what do you want?"

"No, I mean you have a face that could sail a thousand ships kind of beautiful," he counters.

I notice the speedometer inching past 85 miles an hour. "Can you focus on the road please?" I say turning fluorescent pink.

"And that's not even half of it," he says. "You are really powerful. I can feel it."

"Will you please stop flirting with me? It's really awkward."

"I'm not flirting." He says, "I am focusing on how you really are. If I can see you this way, it will allow me to see these parts in myself. We are connected." The car is speeding upwards of 95 miles an hour, and a siren goes off behind us.

"Oh no!" I say shoving my hands over my face.

"It's okay. I've got this," he says pulling over.

The cop walks up behind the car whistling. "Wooohee! I clocked you at 95 miles an hour." He is heavy-set with a thick black mustache and his voice carries the faint echo of a southern drawl. He leans his arm on the door, and stars at my legs. I pull my sweatshirt down over my knees.

"License and registration," he coughs.

"It's a good thing you are here officer," Patrick swoons. I can see a shift in the cop's eyes as Patrick speaks. "If I'm speeding, I need to learn this lesson and you are best man for the job."

The officer looks like he is in a trance. He smiles and copies down Patrick's name and driver's license number. "This will go on your file with a warning. I trust there won't be any more speeding." The officer hands Patrick his license, smiles, and taps the car door before he walks back to his vehicle and drives off.

"What was that?" I demand. "Did you just charm your way out of a ticket?"

"That was not easy." Patrick says pulling the car onto the highway, "It's hard to see the good in people when they are being slime balls."

"I know right? He was super creepy," I say pulling my hair from out of my sweatshirt. "I can't believe he didn't give you a ticket."

Surprisingly, Patrick looks worried. "He wrote down my name and license plate number," he says.

"So? You didn't get a ticket hoodini," I say.

"You're right. It's probably no big deal," he says smiling, "But I definitely should have let you drive."

"It's a learning robot!" I say poking his arm. "Now seriously, how did you not get a ticket going 95 miles an hour?"

"Okay. But promise not to look at me funny."

"I promise."

"It's called wave interference encoding," he says. "There are fields of energy all around humans, all around everything, and when I see things a certain way they are forced to respond to this influence. So I saw that guy as the kindest, most benevolent human on Earth. Kind of a challenge considering he was being a tool." He points a finger at me, "You promised!"

"What?" I say.

"Don't look at me like that," he says.

"Alright, I'm sorry," I say. "I can't control my face. It's why I'm such a bad liar."

"It's okay. You wear your emotions on your sleeve," he says pulling into a diner. "Let's eat."

A 1950's jukebox is playing "That'll Be the Day" and a row of red-pleather booths line the front window. We slide into one of the booths and a blonde waitress with a name tag labeled "KAYLA" takes our order.

"Two waters?" she asks, biting her pen and digesting Patrick with her eyes.

"Water would be good," he says looking over the menu.

The menu is covered in different combinations of grease, fried onions, burgers, bacon, with more bacon and extra grease on the side. I drool over the pepperjack cheeseburger with extra pickles and sweet potato fries and order a salad without any croutons or dressing.

"That's right," I say. "No dressing."

"I'll have the double bacon reuben burger with extra mayo and a side of onion rings and a chocolate shake with whipped cream," Patrick says.

"Wow," she says flirtatiously. "Somebody's hungry. I'll have that right out."

"No dressing really?" he chides. "Are you some kind of squirrel or rabbit?"

"No, I just have really sensitive food allergies to pretty much everything."

"Me too!" He confides.

"Really?"

"No," he says. "I eat whatever I want as long as I want it. You just gotta love it, and it will be good for you."

I contemplate this as the waitress brings our order. She gives Patrick his grease plate and hands me a cheeseburger with extra pickles and sweet potato fries. "I didn't order this, I say."

"Oh, I'm sorry. I wrote it down word for word." Kayla looks confused.

"It's okay, I'll try it," I say.

I look at Patrick inhaling an onion ring. "How did she know I really wanted this?" I say.

"I don't know – maybe she's psychic," he says lifting his eyebrow. "That is good stuff right there."

I look at the fries and contemplate the situation: if I eat these and have an allergic reaction it will be a major detour on the trip, but I want to test Patrick's theory. I don't know if I want to prove him right or wrong, but I definitely want to test it.

"I'm going to eat this." Patrick drops the onion ring and looks intently into my eyes. I am frozen by the look in his eyes and find myself unable to look away.

"You can do this. The potato and you come from the same place – so it can't hurt you. This is no big deal. I promise." I break the chain of focus connecting us and hold back the urge to laugh at him. I take a deep breath and decide to trust this crazy boy. I breathe and contemplate the fry laying on the edge of my plate as being pure wholesome goodness, and take a bite. At first I sense my tongue swelling up, but before the panic fully sets in, I redirect my attention to seeing myself as part potato – literally, me and the potato, like one happy unit. Slowly, the swelling goes down. It seriously goes down. I let out a small squeal and I take another bite. Before long, the entire cheeseburger is devoured, and we are, in the end, one.

"Slow down tiger," Patrick laughs. "There's more in the back I'm sure."

"I can't believe I ate this!" I say smiling. "I love the fatty goodness. I will eat it in the park and I will eat it in the dark..."

"With a fox? On a box?" Patrick jokes as he pays the bill.

"I always thought I was super allergic but I was wrong," I say shaking my head.

"I think some people really are allergic, but I sensed not so much with you. You had a serious mind-block on that one. What made you think you couldn't eat ... well, pretty much anything?"

"My mom."

"Oh," he says raising both eyebrows and nodding his head slowing. "You have one of those too," he adds with a smile.

Feeling like I deserve a gold medal, or at least one of those fancy blue ribbons, I strut to the back of the restaurant to find the restroom. On the way I pass Kayla whose eyes are intent upon making their way back to Patrick. She pretends she doesn't see me, and I manage to find the restroom around the corner.

Even the door is covered in grease. The bathroom light flickers off and on and I breathe a deep sigh of relief. Maybe this trip wasn't such a bad idea after all. As I push on the door to the stall anticipating the probability of finding toilet paper, I jump back as a tall man with an icy smile pushes his way out of the stall. A second more formidable figure protrudes out of the adjacent stall.

"I'm sorry. I should have looked at the sign." I say, turning quickly to exit the room.

"Where is your boyfriend? You are both coming with us little missy." A gruff voice echoes across the tile and cement.

I can feel his fingers grip my arm as I turn and notice a drop of water slowly form into a tiny but clear reflection of the room, and fill nearly to the point of falling from the faucet in the sink. My legs move with complete ease as I race to open the door, and I watch the two men scramble after me. I watch them in slow motion and wait long enough to slam the taller man's face into the door. I see the outline of Patrick's hair outside the window, and I can feel my own pace slowing as I slam into the hard thick glass of the front door, and yank on the handle.

"Get in the car!" I shout as a thin black arrow flashes by my head. Another one skirts past my leg. I turn to see the two men bursting out of the restaurant with what look like bow-guns, shooting at us.

Chapter 4

I feel every hair on my body stand up, and before I know it I'm in the front seat of the car. Patrick rolls across the pavement doing a somersault, averting two arrows that slam with dull thuds into the car. I am shocked to see him stand up and face the men.

He laughs as he calls out to them, "Hey you bumbling idiots! You couldn't tie your shoe! Have fun tripping on that rock, you little babies."

My jaw drops as the men actually fall over each other and one of them appears to have been shot in the leg by the other. Patrick steps back into the car, and in seconds we are driving back onto the highway.

"What just happened? Who were they? Why are people shooting arrows at us? What did you do?" I can't get enough air in my lungs and the questions fly out almost as fast as the arrows that just missed my face.

"Calm down. Try breathing for a change. I'll tell you everything," Patrick orders.

"But there were men trying to shoot us. They have bow-gun things," I gasp. "Shooting at us," I say panicking.

"Yea, but they can't aim." He laughs. "As long as we see them as inept, bumbling idiots they will have a really hard time hitting us. I always picture them as little children playing or adorable and harmless creatures – like hamsters. They are nothing to be afraid of, trust me."

"Trust you?" I yell counting the issues on my fingers. "First, you invite me on a road trip to somewhere I don't even know. B, you drive like stunt man and get pulled over and then, and here's the clincher, and this has to be like number six, you act like it's totally fun to get shot at. Ally was right. I'm gonna die. Oh, yea. And number eleven – and this part is really good, my mom doesn't even know where I am. So I'm like triple dead times a hundred. Take me home. Right now. Just turn around."

"You really need to study up on the math," he says. I blink my eyes at him vacantly, no longer comprehending what words he is speaking. I seriously wonder what planet he came from. "You know, it was a mistake, letting that guy take my name. I shouldn't have got pulled over." Patrick laments and hitting the steering wheel. "He took my name and license number. Why did I let him have it?"

"So what?" I ask bewildered.

Patrick sighs. "The Valencia access all police records," he says. "I stole a scroll from them two years ago, and let's just say that did not make them happy."

"The Valencia? You stole something from who?" I ask. Then I remember, I want to live. "Take me home right now," I demand.

"I know this seems crazy. And I'm sorry you are involved. But I think you would be anyway. The Valencia make a habit out of controlling the paranormal, and they would have found you eventually. Now it is even more important that we make it to New Mexico. They won't be able to follow us after we reach Entael, and if we turn around now it won't be long before they track us down."

"The paranormal? I am not the para normal. I am the normal normal."

He looks directly into my eyes. "You are far more powerful than you think, and it's about time you figured that out."

I run my fingers through my hair to calm my thoughts, and attempt to view the world according to Patrick.

"So, the bad guys are minions from a group called the 'Valencia' and we are headed where?"

"To Entael, a sacred space hidden in the mountains of New Mexico, it is protected."

"Why should I trust you? There were hundreds of arrows flying right at me," I say just for the sake of argument.

"And not a single one of them hit you. What are the odds do you think?"

"That was just luck," I reply.

"Just like it was just luck when you ran across two tennis courts?"

I breathe a deep sigh. Patrick shifts gears and takes hold of my hand. Somehow I actually feel safe. I feel more powerful than I've ever felt in my life.

"I promise you are safe. I'm on the good side, Amy."

I find myself nodding my head even though the mom voice inside is still telling me to turn the car around. "We can't stay on the main highway," I say.

"If we take the scenic route we will be there by night fall," he says as we pull onto a back-road with a sign that says "Garden of the Gods next right".

Patrick takes a sharp curve climbing up a hill and my heart threatens to jump out of my chest.

"Do you think you could slow down and enjoy the ride?" I ask as I brace my arms ready to fall off the cliff.

"I am enjoying the ride. But I can go slow," he says looking over to see me bracing the door like a cat in a bathtub.

The scenery has shifted to sand colored stones jetting straight up amongst sage and cedar trees. Beyond the desert lies the dark horizon of a smoky-lavender mountain.

"This area is surreal," I say

"Some say it's magical," he replies

I take out my vitamins and open "Saturday."

"Those are some huge pills. I didn't know you did drugs," he jokes.

"Yea, that's me, the pill pusher. You want some vitamin D?" I laugh.

"No thanks. But I'd take my chances with some of those Cracker Jacks," he suggests.

"Alright," I say, opening the box. "But you're going to answer some questions."

"So this is an interrogation?" He smiles seductively. "I'm in."

"What is happening to me when everything slows down?" I ask and toss a Cracker Jack in the direction of his mouth.

His mouth opens to catch it, and he crunches while he answers, "I don't know exactly. But it has something to do with your perception. When you look at the world, you create a sort of holographic image, literally perceiving solid shapes. But in truth, these shapes are solidified by your perception of them. When you shift your perception of everything around you, everything around you responds to this."

This all sounds a little hoogie-woogie to me, and I wonder what kind of drugs Patrick has taken. Patrick scoffs at my hesitation and replies, "Ana knows way more than I do. You can ask her that one."

"Okay," I say, popping another Cracker Jack toward his mouth to console him. "What is the scroll you took and why did you steal it?"

Patrick mumbles through the crunching. "It was a translation of the Indus script. It showed how we can communicate without words. The Valencia wanted to keep it secret. They want to keep everything awesome a secret. They are such douchballs."

"So can you communicate without words?"

I feel an image of triangle with a line through it resonating in my head and sense the words "of course."

"How did you do that?" I look over at him astonished.

"You'll see," he laughs. "What happened to the sugar bribe?"

I toss a few more Cracker Jacks and he catches them like a seal at Sea World.

"If we can translate our thoughts through images, we will be able to talk to anyone in the world," I say. "No more separation between people. This is really important. We have to share this."

"It's not that simple, Amy. This is a sacred practice. It takes us back to a space before language, and some people aren't ready for that. Their identities could get lost."

I give him a look. Somehow his answer seems like something an adult would say. It's just talking without words. What could go wrong?

I can tell he doesn't want to talk about it (ironic, I know,) and I decide to let it go. The sun is beginning to set behind the mountain, and I can feel the butterflies rising in my stomach. I'm nervous. Patrick looks over and puts his arm around my neck.

"It's going to be okay," he says. "Don't be scared. You are going to love this place. But in order for this to work, you need to focus your thoughts on what you want."

"I don't know what I want."

"Okay, repeat after me. We are going to reach Entael. We are going to feel great."

I sit up and try, "We are going to reach Entael. We are going to feel great."

"I am totally open to all the awesome possibilities that lay before us," he says

Trying not to imagine myself at a self-help seminar, I repeat, "I am totally open to all the awesome possibilities that lay before us."

Surprisingly, something shifts inside and the butterflies are gone. Instead there is a warm glow and everything looks softer somehow. The desert gleams in the sunlight and all of my apprehension melts into pure excitement.

Patrick continues, "I love when Patrick doesn't shave. He is super-hot." I laugh and punch his arm.

Patrick looks in the rearview mirror and his smile fades. "Someone is following us," he says in shock.

I turn around to see a dark army-green Jeep behind us. Patrick takes a sharp left and the Jeep follows. We narrowly miss a giant boulder as we careen off the dirt path doubling back to the main road. The Jeep skids in the dirt and turns back to follow us. I feel the warm cozy feeling dissipating into another adrenaline rush.

The car is speeding up the mountain at ninety-miles an hour, and I try to take a deep breath. In my mind I repeat "the possibilities that lay before us are totally awesome" over and over. I try to picture us driving off peacefully into the sunset, but as the Jeep gets closer, the panic sets in and makes itself at home in my stomach.

"I love car chases!" Patrick says as he accelerates around a corner. He seems to be enjoying himself, which as I look over the cliff flying below, somehow doesn't make me feel better. "Hold on, I've got to shake this guy!" he shouts.

Patrick takes a sharp right and I brace the window as the car rolls upside down. I can feel time slow, and somehow I feel calm. I see the Jeep keep going straight off the cliff, and notice the navigation screen blinking before a giant explosion of white fabric shoves me back into the seat. There is silence as I look over to see Patrick passed-out in the driver's seat. I reach my hand over to open my door, and roll out of the car to stand upright. Amazingly, I can't sense any serious pain. Everything seems fine except for the bruise on my chest from the seat-belt. I walk around the front of the car and yank the door open to see Patrick slouched motionless with a cut on his forehead.

"Patrick! Wake up!" I shout, shaking his chest.

His eyes slowly open. He grimaces rubbing his forehead.

"Let's get you out of here."

I pull him out of the car and we survey the damage. The car is completely wrecked. The sun has now set below the horizon and I shiver slightly as I survey the landscape.

"Are you okay?" he asks

"Yea, I'm fine. Are you okay?"

"I have a headache, but I'll be fine. I better go check on those guys," he says motioning over the cliff.

We walk over to the edge of the cliff and see Jeep pieces scattered down the ledge. Patrick jumps onto a boulder and makes his way to the where most of the Jeep is intact. I check my phone and realize we need to call 911. Whoever those men were, they are still human, and they deserve help. After a surprising hold on the emergency line, I finally get through and explain the situation. I tell the operator we were being chased and may be in danger. She warns us to wait for help, and I reiterate that they need to hurry. Patrick surfaces from examining the drivers and lets the operator know that both drivers are knocked unconscious. We turn to hear a rumbling noise down in the valley, and see eight wild horses coming up the canyon toward us.

They all have white diamond markings on their foreheads, and thick fur around their hooves. Three tan, three dark brown, and two spotted white, they breathe heavily as the pound across the desert floor. Their manes roll in waves and their eyes are alive with an intensity I haven't seen in horses before.

Patrick tells the operator, "No, we aren't staying here. We are safe, but will be leaving the scene of the accident shortly," he says and hangs up the phone.

"Are those Mustangs?" I ask

"Those are my friends."

Coming up the hill at full speed, they pour onto the landing where we stand. Eight majestic creatures moving in short bursts, try to slow down from the sprint up the hill. They stomp the dust and stare at me. In the haze of the dust cloud I see the form of one of the tan horses shift, and in the next second, a tall woman with long blonde hair stands before us. Amazingly she is wearing cowboy boots, chaps over her jeans and a wool sweater.

"Hello Elaine," Patrick walks forward and embraces the woman, "it's so good to see you."

Chapter 5

"We came as soon as we sensed you were in danger." Elaine flashes a brilliant smile of gleaming white teeth. Her voice is warm and inviting. "Aren't you going to introduce me?" she asks.

I know that the normal response would be to smile, shake her hand and introduce myself. But I just witnessed this woman transform from being a horse, and normal just isn't happening right now. I stand there staring at her in disbelief, wondering if she is real.

"This is Amy," Patrick explains. "Amy Kitcher."

"Pleased to meet you," Elaine reaches to shake my hand. The other horses – or people? watch me as they pace. Elaine's hand grasps my own and I can feel her pulse. I relax slightly, knowing she is an actual human, sort of.

"I'm sorry," I say trying to hide my astonishment, "did you just transform from a horse, into a human?"

"Elaine is a Nektosha," Patrick says. "A shape shifter..."

"For generations we have honored the wild horse. They are our kin, and at times we roam these hills free of the trappings of man," Elaine proudly explains. "It is a secret I trust you to keep."

Elaine's eyes stare with resolve and I nod my head and manage to say, "of course."

"We need to make tracks before the bad guys wake up or the cops show up," Patrick says urgently.

I blink my eyes trying to process the transformation, as seven horses shift one at a time into seven human figures.

Elaine looks at Patrick, and then at the others, "Amy can ride with me..."

"I suppose since I am the strongest, Patrick should ride with me," the tallest one in the group brags.

"Thanks Brandon, you know I like 'em tall, dark and handsome," Patrick teases him.

"Shut-up man," Brandon commands. Patrick continues laughing. In a flash of an eye, Brandon takes the form of a giant mustang with dark brown hair and two flaming eyes. He rears up, and Patrick balks.

"Okay, brother. I'm sorry," he says putting his hands up in surrender. "Thanks for the ride."

Brandon stands down long enough to let Patrick on, and Elaine and the others have shifted and are stomping the ground in anticipation. I look at Elaine. Her back is almost as tall as I am, and I wonder how I am supposed to get up there without a saddle. She seems to know what I am thinking, and kneels forward to let me on. Just as I get my bearings, and fasten my bag securely to my shoulder, we take off back down the hill.

It is a good thing Elaine has a long mane, because otherwise there would be nothing to hold onto as I wrap my legs as tight as I can hugging her ribs. Traveling downward over the rocky ledge, she struggles to keep her footing. I lean back to help maintain balance. The steps are slow and uneven; a crevasse below jerks me forward and I come dangerously close to losing my grip. I have ridden horses before, and somehow it always seemed okay to put a bridle in their mouth and jab them with my riding boots to get them to move faster. This time however, it is different. Knowing that Elaine is a human makes me think twice about kicking her, and I find myself wondering if she is used to carrying people around. Am I heavy? Am I pulling her hair too hard?

Unfortunately, I can't contemplate these questions, because suddenly we are vaulting at full speed, winding up through the foothills and I can feel my weight slipping back. I lean forward and grasp a thicker hold on her mane, I mean hair. My own hair is flinging around wildly and for a second I lose track of which strands are hers and which are my own. I can hear seven other horses thundering up the hill all around us. I glance over to see Patrick almost get wacked in the head by a tree branch as we make it to the top of the hill and into the cover of

Pinon trees. We finally slow to a stop; Elaine is panting heavily, and I jump down.

"Thank you," I say to her.

She nods her head and walks off into the brush. My legs feel numb and I stumble to a nearby log. I try to stop the world from spinning and to reconcile the sounds in the shadowy darkness. Some kind of coyote, or wolf, howls in the distance.

Patrick jumps down and asks Brandon in disbelief, "do you really want to hurt me?"

Brandon neighs garishly, and you can perceive the faint resemblance to laughter as he runs off down to the creek roaring nearby.

"Are you okay?" Patrick asks. I pause to contemplate this question. Am I okay? So far, we have been pulled over, attacked by strange men in the bathroom, chased down by the same crazy people, wrecked a vehicle and ridden horses that are also people. Okay doesn't really get at what I am feeling right now. "I think we should set up camp and finish the journey in the morning," Patrick comments.

I just look at him. I know my silent treatment is brutal, and I'm letting him have it.

"Are you thirsty?" he asks hopefully.

I turn my head and take out my cell phone. Unbelievably, I still get service. I text a message to my mom: "Ally and I are just watching movies. I'll call you tomorrow."

"Are you mad?" Patrick asks.

I pause for a second. No, not mad, I think to myself. I am just traumatized. I text another message to Ally: "oomm but iag cylt mysm," and look up at Patrick. The pain in my bladder convinces me to break my silent treatment. "I really have to pee," I say desperately.

He laughs. "For a second there, I thought you hated me. Common, let's go find a big rock."

I have to squeeze my knees to hold it together. I'm too overwhelmed to tell Patrick off right now.

We hike up through the rocky terrain and I manage to find a secluded area to emancipate my bladder. I take a couple of long, deep breaths and wonder if Patrick can hear how long this is going on for. It's like a marathon or something. I can hear the sound of neighing horses down by the creek, and wrap my sweatshirt close to my chest in a failed attempt to stay warm. Patrick gathers chunks of wood into a clearing and pulls out a lighter to start a fire.

"Do you smoke?" I ask with curiosity.

"Rarely," he replies, lighting the fire into a full blaze, "usually for a ceremony or vision-quest. Do you?"

"Nope," I reply remembering our situation. "So what's the plan? I trusted you, and here we are in the middle of nowhere, running away from violent men with horse people. It feels like I am sky-diving with a parachute that only works part of the time, and you keep smiling and telling me 'it's all good', while I plunge to my death. It's awesome." I whisper angrily, my arms tense and my eyes glaring, "let me translate: I just texted my friend and my mom, and I told them I was safe, but I don't feel safe. I feel pretty freaked-out, and I just want you to be honest. Am I safe?"

"Honestly?" he says, standing up. "We are pretty safe. The Nektosha will protect us through the night and we will make our way to Entael tomorrow morning." He takes my shoulders in a firm grasp, and looks through the moonlight into my eyes. "If you want to leave, I understand. But at this point, I don't know what the Valencia are after, and until I know for sure they aren't after you, I think we should stick together."

I take a deep breath and start crying. "This is the best-worst day of my life!" I gasp through tear-jerked mumbles. "I don't know what to do, and if I end up dead my mom is going to kill me," I cry. Patrick holds me close enough for me to sob into his chest. I forget for a moment we are in the middle of nowhere and feel the warmth of the fire, the sound of his breathing and his beating heart.

"I'm sorry," he says still holding me. "You are going to be fine, no matter what happens. The parachute will open. I promise."

"Okay," I say, taking a deeper breath and biting my lip. I feel light-headed but calm. The smell of the fire and the woods mingle into a nostalgic image from my childhood, and the panic subsides. The Nektosha return up to the clearing, and six of the eight take their human form and sit by the fire. Elaine sits next to me, while Brandon takes a punch at Patrick's arm.

"Enjoy the ride?" Brandon asks playfully.

"Yea, that was actually kind of fun. Crazy. But fun." Patrick replies. "In all the years I've known you, I've never taken a ride."

A woman across the fire laughs. "You never asked."

The guy next to her replies, "I have definitely asked."

There is mixed laughter, as I stand. "We haven't been introduced," I reach over and extend my hand to meet everyone. Brandon shakes my arm vigorously, with a large grin. Maria, a short tan woman with dark braids waves and smiles easily at me but then glances back flirtatiously at Patrick. Jay and Rick nod their heads preferring to maintain some distance.

"My name is Aaron," the boy next to Maria reaches out to shake my hand. He takes a few short breaths as if he is sniffing my arm and I pull back uncomfortably. "You smell good," he smiles innocently. His nose and jaw drop forward slightly, and he vaguely resembles the white mustang I witnessed climbing up the hill. The group laughs a little and settles into silence with eyes gazing into the fire.

"So what happened on the canyon?" Elaine asks.

"We were being chased by Valencia thugs. They went after Amy earlier in the restroom –

"I still can't believe I went in the wrong bathroom," I moan.

Patrick continues, "I don't know what they are after, but we were headed to Entael."

"That's less than a day trip." Elaine offers, "We can take you tomorrow." The rest nod their heads in affirmation.

Patrick looks at me, and I nod slightly. "That would be great," he says enthusiastically.

I lean against Patrick, and within an hour we are all laying down in a circle around the fire. Patrick wraps his arms around my shoulder to keep me warm. The two remaining Nektosha stand on the periphery, their tails flicking periodically, just near the halo of the firelight. I drift into a deep sleep.

———-

I wake to a cacophony of birds chattering before dawn. "The sun isn't even up yet," I say. "What do they have to talk about this early?"

Patrick rolls over and yawns. "The blue jay over there is pissed off because that is his tree, and there's a woodpecker who is drilling in it for sap. There's also bunch of chickadees who just like to talk."

"Can you ask them to keep it down?" I ask, half serious.

Patrick whistles a poor imitation of the blue jay. The bird pauses for a moment, and then keeps pestering the woodpecker. "He probably thinks we are the weird ones." Patrick says.

"Well he's right about one of us." I say joking. There's a part of me that is a little surprised he can't talk to animals given the events of the past 24 hours, but I really can't blame him for trying. It's better than just complaining about them. "Okay, I'm up," I say rolling over to press my hands into the blanket of pine needles. My back cracks as I do a push up, and I will my eyes to open.

Patrick follows suit, and we laugh weakly at the pain of sleeping in the woods. It is a bittersweet feeling of accomplishment, and it feels good to be so close to the Earth for a change. The others have already risen, and I can see the outline of two of the Nektosha down by the creek. Patrick cracks his back and we make our way to the ledge where we watch the sunrise.

"Where are we?" I ask, watching the rolls of light sweep across the sky. There is a soft breeze, and with the exception of the birds, it is deeply quiet.

"We are in the Rio Grande National Forest," he replies. "About six hours on foot from Entael."

"And you are sure we'll be safe there?" I ask.

"Positive."

We watch as the clouds bloom into hot glowing flames across the sky. Soon the sun is fully-risen, and the clouds lighten to a soft cover of white. The others are starting to gather. Elaine is in her human form and has her hair pulled back in a braid. Aaron and Maria walk back up from the creek, while Brandon is doing a set of push-ups on a nearby boulder. The other four remain in their horse form, and one of them is intent on scratching his head on an aspen tree.

"We should get going. It is a beautiful day for a run." Elaine smiles brightly.

"I figure we have about six hours left on foot," Patrick estimates.

"It's less if you ride." Maria replies, smiling intently at Patrick.

"Amy – do you want to ride?" Patrick looks at me uncertain about this prospect. I'm still a bit uneasy about riding the Nektosha, but if it means getting to safety faster I figure it's worth the awkwardness.

"Sure," I say half-smiling.

"Great! I'll take Patrick." Maria exclaims excitedly.

"I can take Amy," Brandon beams.

I look over at Patrick. I know we aren't a couple, and I really shouldn't care which of the Nektosha he rides, but I am definitely feeling a little uncomfortable with this situation. Am I really getting jealous? I push the twisted feeling in my chest just beneath awareness. Denial seems possible right now.

"Okay," I say with false confidence.

Patrick looks back at me before he turns to face Maria. "Are you sure I'm not too heavy?" he asks.

"You have no idea how strong I can be," Maria chides him before taking her horse form.

I smile a little uneasily at Brandon, whose teeth gleam in the morning sunlight, which makes his skin look golden. As he takes his horse-shape, I notice his fur remains the same dark brown color as his human hair. He kneels quickly and I jump up. I try to rationalize this experience: He's a nice guy. No big deal. This is like getting a piggy-back ride from friends when I was little. It's just now we are trekking across a national forest, and the friend is a larger, more furry species. This is cool, I think to myself. But I can't help feeling a little awkward as I grasp his mane for balance.

I look over at Patrick who is falling behind the group. If this is not a big deal, then why do I feel jealous? In her horse form, Maria has the same dark eyes that seem to sparkle under the shadows, and I can see Patrick's face gazing peacefully across the horizon. Why does he always seem so relaxed and content? I feel my inner parachute falter a bit, and decide to focus on the scenery.

Thousands of aspen trees envelope us as we cantor along a faintly worn path; I can feel a warm pulse, as if they are alive. I look up the hill of trees to see a black bear running across the top of the hill. I turn to point him out to Patrick, but he is too far behind. His front paws pounce the earth playfully; swerving through the trees, his shadow flickers down the hillside through the trees. Although he prances like a cub, I can tell, even from where we ride, this is no small creature. He heaves heavy, deep grunts as he gallops alongside us across the ridge, and finally turns to go down the other side of the hill.

We ride for at least four hours, before I picture the image of a wavy line running to a circle, and sense the words "Are you okay?" I look back to see Patrick questioning me with his eyes. I grimace slightly, and manage a weak smile as a shrug my shoulders as if to say "sort of." I picture another symbol, this time a dash with a line running perpendicular down the middle, followed by a second dash. I sense the meaning, "we will be stopping soon."

We come to a stream, and the Nektosha come to a stop. I jump down, and welcome the ground beneath my feet. I see Maria talking with Patrick down the stream, and turn to see Brandon flashing his league of piercing white teeth.

"What a beautiful day," he says happily.

"Thanks for the ride," I reply. "It is really beautiful here."

I wonder if anyone else saw the black bear racing us through the forest, when I see Maria reach up to kiss Patrick on the cheek.

"It's no problem," I hear her saying. "It is my pleasure." I can hear Patrick ask her where I am, and I feel a slight release of the tension in my chest, as he makes his way toward us.

The Nektosha have all taken their human form, and Elaine leans her arm around my shoulders. "It has been a pleasure meeting you," she says warmly. "I hope we meet again."

"It has been really great meeting you all" I say, looking at everyone except Maria. "Thank you so much."

"We should be able to make it easily from here," Patrick says to Elaine. He hugs her, and shakes all of the guy's hands. Maria leans in for a hug, and I feel a selfish pang of satisfaction as Patrick reaches out his hand for a less-than romantic farewell.

Watching the Nektosha ride back through the forest, Patrick brags, "we are about an hour away on foot from Entael," with an "I told you so" kind of tone, while trying to pull a fist bump.

"Yay!" I reply sarcastically returning his all too platonic fist bump, and trying to hide my desire for something a little more romantic.

Chapter 6

We walk along the faintly worn path quickly at first, anticipating the destination, and I notice Patrick is collecting dark purple flowers from bushes along the path. "What are you doing?" I ask, wondering if this is lunch.

"We are almost to the Entael. It is your first time, and if you don't eat these you won't be able to see it."

"Won't be able to see it? Come on." I demand. "What is it?" I ask with my last effort at patience.

"They help you to wake up and see what is actually there. If you don't eat it, and haven't been to Entael before, you will see it as just another part of the forest."

"Are you kidding? I'm supposed to eat these flowers, which will make me see invisible stuff? This sounds like a drug, and I don't really feel like tripping out and hallucinating some place."

"Amy, I'm not trying to drug you. In small doses this flower is perfectly safe. The Entael exists on a higher plane of vibration, and you literally won't see it if you haven't been meditating for days or have taken this flower. Come on Amy, I've taken you this far. You've got to trust me," Patrick implores, looking a little desperate.

"How long do the effects last?" I ask.

"Not long, an hour, maybe two."

I take two of the blooms from his open hand. Long, dark purple petals envelope bright yellow stamens; they taste spicy, almost like pepper. Patrick smiles and shakes his head at me. I am apparently a handful. My mouth is trying against my will to spit out the flowers, and I forcefully swallow the crushed flowers. I find myself smacking my tongue to get rid of the taste. "Okay, I did it," I say proudly.

"Good job. Now you can have dessert," he jokes.

We start walking again along the gently worn path. I notice the sun pouring down through the trees, the leaves flicker in the sunlight like diamonds. The soft harmony of the birds calling each other is complemented by the sound of the air rushing across the sky. Everything is alive, and it is all connected. Patrick looks more content than I've ever seen him, and his hair bounces playfully in the breeze. I can feel a soft vibration on my tongue and it feels as though an electrical pulse is running throughout my entire body. The ground feels soft, and I sense a deep feeling of love for every piece of dirt below us. My pace is slower than I normally would walk, and I feel myself wanting to stop and just take it all in. Everything seems so completely new, like I've never seen any of it before.

"Don't slow down too much," Patrick leans his arm around my shoulders. "We want to make it in time for lunch."

I smile from deep inside out of pure enjoyment. "But it's so beautiful." I sit down on a boulder and run my fingers gently along the fibers of stone. Even the rock seems alive.

Patrick is laughing so hard he is holding his stomach as he tries to explain. "You are really cute you know that? I know it's really beautiful, and I would love to sit here with you and commune with this amazing planet, but we really have to keep walking." He takes my hand and pulls me back onto the path.

We walk on and I find myself welling up inside, as if I could cry from all of the beauty. My body feels completely electric, as warm vibrations pulse throughout my veins. The energy in my chest is spinning and I've never felt so light and free. On the downside, the lightness has pretty much taken over my head, and I feel like I could pass out. I find myself leaning on Patrick slightly as we walk up the hill. As we reach the top of the hill I see it: a collection of seven domes. One in the center with a glass ceiling and six others nestled around it forming a perfect circle. They are all white, made of stucco, and I notice each one has a different roof. I have never seen any architectural structure like it in my life.

"We're here," Patrick breathes a sigh of relief. "Welcome to Entael."

"It's so beautiful," I say as tears break free and stream down my cheeks.

We walk down the hill and approach what must be the front entrance. Patrick turns the latch on a thick set of wooden doors which open to reveal a room full of stained glass. A pattern starts at the top of the ceiling with tiny red and yellow squares oscillating into blue, green and purple as the squares rotate into loops swooping down the sides of the room. The colored light creates a soft haze on the tile below, and I notice the same pattern is echoed on the floor, except the loops extend to form a circle in the center of the room.

"Pretty cool uh?" Patrick nudges my arm. I stand completely silent, lingering in the entrance, and sense a deep sacred energy circulating through the room. "The pattern is based on the Fibonacci sequence," Patrick comments. "It is the pattern of nature."

A tall woman with curly dark hair approaches us smiling. "You made it," she says hugging Patrick. "I was beginning to worry."

Patrick introduces us. "This is my friend Amy Kitcher. Amy, this is my mom, Ana."

Did he just say his mom? My mind comes back into focus as I find the right words. "Pleased to meet you," I finally say extending hand.

Her eyes have a steady gaze, and reflect the same color of green that I've come to know in Patrick's eyes. "A pleasure to meet you," she says with a warm grasp of my hand. "You must be hungry after the trip?" I nod my head in confirmation, a little grateful someone recognized the growling in my belly. "Let's get you some food," she says escorting us across the dance of color and light of the curved room.

She pushes open another wooden door to reveal a second dome of light, this time covered in clear glass. The room is the exact same size as the first dome, but it is filled with the twists and turns of branches climbing up to the sunlight. The trunk of a magnificent tree rises from the center of the dome into a cloud of branches. I breathe the warm air that smells of vegetation, and I am again struck in silent wonder, as the leaves reverberate and reflect against the glass dome, I can hear the sound of birds, and see several windows at the top of the dome left open. It almost feels as if the clouds outside are drifting in through the window.

"We call this old girl the Tree of Life," Patrick speaks quietly. I can tell this is a sacred space by the reverence in his tone, and the quiet way they walk under the shade of the tree. Huge roots protrude out of the ground, and I realize we are walking on stones embedded in the earth beneath our feet.

"All of the rooms here are connected by this space," Patrick says pointing out six doors evenly spaced around the room. We walk to the one straight across from the door we came in. "This one is the living quarters."

Ana leads us through to the left of yet another dome space, where a group of people sit at various tables eating lunch. Several of them smile at us and I feel compelled to wave at an older man with a long white beard and a twinkle in his eyes. A line of food is left on a buffet table.

"Hmmmm. Lentils." Patrick says less than enthused.

I pour a giant glass of water and drink it down only to pour another one. We sit down to eat spicy lentil curry, and I am full of questions. "So what is this place? Where did it come from?"

"We aren't sure when it was built, but the Entael is a sacred space. Spiritual masters from all over the world come here for retreat, and to commune with each other," Ana says. It is not known to the public, but it is open to friends who seek the truth. I have been coming ever since I was pregnant with Patrick," she says pinching his cheek.

"My mom is a quantum physicist. She came here to study the consciousness of highly developed spiritual masters, and then she started turning into one herself," Patrick jokes.

"Yes, well, it has been a bit of a journey," Ana laughs heartily. "Speaking of journeys, how was yours?" I expected you yesterday..."

"Fine if you don't count the Valencia thugs who came after us," Patrick says. "What do they want? I thought you gave them back their precious scroll."

"I did give it back. Patrick, what have you done now?"

"Nothing mom, I swear. I've just been hanging out with dad and going to school."

"I made an agreement with Luca, that he would leave you alone if I turned over the scroll. He should have honored that pact," she says leaning over to touch Patrick's arm. "I will get to the bottom of this, but you have to promise me you didn't steal anything else or taunt them in any way."

"I don't know what their problem is. They are such tools. They tried to take Amy, and they were using darts with some kind of sedative. They wanted to take us both alive for some reason." Patrick says, the anger rising in his voice.

"Amy, I'm so sorry. Can I talk to my son in private?" Ana asks impatiently. She stands up and escorts Patrick to a cluster of what look like paper walls across the room. I sit for a few moments wondering what they are saying, and realize I really need to use a restroom. I wonder toward the kitchen area looking for a sign that says Women, when I hear their voices talking.

"Why did you bring her into this mess?" Ana asks sharply. "You know better. She is just an innocent bystander. I am so disappointed in your judgment young man."

"Mom, you don't understand. Amy is special. I really like her. And how was I supposed to know the Valencia would be after us?"

"You know it is always a possibility. We can't trust them right now, not with Luca in charge," Ana's says with concern.

"We are fine. And I had to bring Amy – I think she might be a coder."

"A coder. Really?" she asks with interest. "Well, it still puts her and Entael in danger, and it's all the more reason to not come down here by yourselves. You know they want to keep all coders under their watch." Ana's voice drops to a whisper, "I think she might be closer than we think."

I realize that she is talking about me, and I walk slowly in surrender around the corner with a shadow of shame spread across my face. "I'm so sorry, I didn't mean to—"

"It's okay," Ana interrupts me. "If I had just been through what you have been through, and were in a strange place and people were talking, I would want to hear them too." I relax the tension in my jaw and breathe a deep sigh of relief. "I'm just concerned about your safety."

Ana turns to Patrick, "I want you both to stay in Entael until I speak with Luca."

"Okay mom. It's not like we can go too far. I wrecked my car," Patrick confesses.

"You wrecked your car! Does your father know?" Ana exclaims loudly with her hand permanently clenching her forehead. I can tell she has exceeded the decibel for normal conversation and a few of the patrons savoring a late lunch look over with some mild curiosity.

Patrick implores in a loud whisper, "the Valencia were after us. I had to lose them. It's really not technically my fault."

Ana inhales deeply and blows out an extremely long exhale. "Okay, I really need to meditate. I think we all do. Patrick, why don't you take Amy to her living space and I'll meet you guys for dinner," she says. She approaches me with a look of sympathy. "Everything is going to be alright. I'm going to get to the bottom of this okay?"

"Okay," I say trying to sound as cheery as possible.

Ana approaches Patrick. She looks him squarely in the face with loving frustration as she grasps his head shaking it slightly. She says in slow exasperation, "What am I going to do with you?" As she walks toward the front of the room I can hear her say, "I thought the first born was supposed to be easy."

"Well that went well." Patrick says sarcastically.

"I would say you got off scot-free once again," I chide him. "Look," I say seriously, "I didn't mean to spy on you. I really need to find a restroom."

Patrick laughs and nods his head, "I see. You aren't a femme fatale secret agent – just a poor girl always lookin to go pee."

"That sounds right," I say squirming to contain the water balloon that is about to burst inside me. "Can we make sure it's the ladies room please? I ask only half joking.

Patrick leads me through a maze of thin, paper walls with black spiraling lines which lead us to a door with no sign on it. "It's co-gender," he says smiling. I gratefully occupy the room to relieve myself. The room is covered in tiny tiles that sweep across the stucco wall to form a wave. Scattered across the wave are tiles with tiny symbols on them. I notice several showers around the corner, reviving a memory of smelling like a human.

After exiting the co-gender restroom, I tell Patrick earnestly, "I can't believe you didn't tell me we were coming to see your mom."

"I didn't mention that?"

"No, you didn't." I say crossing my arms.

"Does it really matter?" he asks.

I have to think about it for a moment. There are lots of reasons to be mad at Patrick right now, but this isn't really one of them. "No, I guess it doesn't really matter, but you still should have told me." I take out my phone thinking about my own mother, and how if she knew what I'd been through, how completely freaked out she would be. "No service," I say. I turn to Patrick, "I know your mom told us to stay here, but I have to call my mom and my friend Ally.

"No problem," Patrick replies. "We can take a walk. I think there's service up by the road."

We exit through the living quarters dome into brilliant white sunlight and make our way up the hill. I notice several pools of hot steaming water.

"Are those pools of hot water?" I ask.

"They are called hot springs. Heated by the Earth's core, they naturally happen all around this area. We used to sneak out when I was a kid and come down here with some of the older monks for a soak," Patrick explains.

We come to a road and finally I have enough service to attempt a call to my friend Ally.

The phone rings so many times I almost give up when I hear her voice, "Amy? Where are you? Are you okay?"

"I'm fine. A little freaked out, but I'm here," I say realizing that I promised not to tell anyone about where I actually am. "We are just staying in a hotel down in Santa Fe."

"Why are you 'out of your mind'?" Ally asks with concern.

I notice Patrick walking up the road with his phone dialing someone. I hesitate before answering.

"Is it because of that guy? Peter? Because I will come down there and—" Ally demands.

"No, no, it's not Patrick. He's fine. I actually kind of like him," I say cautiously.

"I know. That's what's got me worried," Ally responds. "If you didn't like him, there wouldn't be any problems."

"Ummm, there are still some problems," I say.

"Okay, just tell me," Ally pleads. "I'm all ears."

I think about telling her. I want to tell her everything, but somehow I know she will completely come unglued and there won't be any way to calm her down 1200 miles away. "I totally forgot my deodorant, my sunglasses, extra socks, my i-pad, and my jacket." I say with a pang of guilt in my chest.

"That is no problem. Do you want me to send you a care-package?" she asks. "I can get most of that stuff in the mail by tomorrow."

"No it's okay, it's only a week. I think I'll manage, and I can buy some deodorant if it gets too bad," I joke.

"Okay, just let me know," she says with all the nurturing elements a best friend should have. I'm really a bad person for lying to her.

"Listen, I gotta go. The service here is terrible. I'll call you in a couple of days," I say.

"You better, or I'll start to freak out."

"I know. I love you," I say.

"I love you too," she answers hanging up.

One down, I think. I start walking down the road and call my mom. I really need to hear her voice but instead I get sent to voice mail. "Hi mom, just wanted to check in. Ally and I are having a blast," I lie. "Miss you so much." I pause listening to the echo of silence before I disconnect from the call, and feel my heart disconnect from the two people I care for the most. I want so much to tell them both, and to be near them right now. What am I doing here? None of this is has to invade my life. I can just leave. I think about how I could rent a car and go home as I walk carefully down the winding road on the mountainside.

Chapter 7

I hear the sound of running footsteps as Patrick rounds the corner chasing after me.

"Hey wait up!" he shouts. "Where are you going?"

"I don't know," I say slowing my pace and turning toward him.

Patrick is out of breath, and bent over trying to catch it. "We should ... get ... back," he says panting.

"I need to take my vitamins," I reply.

Patrick raises his eyebrow in exasperation, and wheezes, "Okay, let's go take some vitamins."

We walk slowly up the road back to Entael. I try to distract myself from the lingering guilt of lying to both Ally and my mom by kicking rocks off the ledge. Patrick can't stop staring at the pools of water accumulating in my eyes making it impossible to ignore it. "What's wrong?" he asks.

"I just lied to my mom and my best friend. I put myself in danger and I can't even tell them about it," I confess.

Patrick sighs. "That is rough. My mom was right, it is my fault. You should know I never meant to put you at risk – you are the first person I've..." he hesitates. "You are the first person I've ever wanted to bring here." I look at him intently, letting my eyes return his gaze. "You are special, Amy." He blushes and turns away. "I don't mean to sound like a troll." He groans in frustration, and punts a rock across the valley. I can't help but smile. He is really bad at apologies, but I can tell he wants to make it better. Patrick reluctantly returns my gaze, "I'm so sorry Amy, it just felt like the right thing to do."

"It's okay." I reply looking toward the door to the living quarters at Entael. "If it was just me, if I didn't have anyone else worried for me, I would be totally fine right now. Except ..." I say pulling open the heavy wooden door.

"Except what?" he asks.

"Except I would still really want to shower," I confess. "A long, hot, steamy shower."

"Aye aye, captain," he salutes. "I'll be right back." He takes off toward the labyrinth of paper walls. I walk over to sit at a table with an older woman drinking tea.

"Can I join you?" I ask.

"Of course you can," she responds in a thick Irish accent. "My name's Grace. Pleased to meet you," she says reaching out to shake my hand. Her eyes drift off for a moment while she grasps my palm. "What brings you to Entael?" she asks gently releasing my hand.

"I'm here with Patrick," I reply quietly.

"Oh, that explains it," she chuckles. "I felt you had been through some adventure. Patrick has a habit of causing mischief," she winks nudging my arm. He's quite the rascal that one – always getting into trouble. Cute kid though, could never really be angry with him." I gaze up at the ceiling. The curved lines I'd seen earlier connect to form two intertwined circles. "The moment of creation – a symbol of fertility," she comments. "This is an ancient reminder that we come from the same place. It is perhaps fitting it is here we house the living quarters."

Patrick approaches the table with an armful of shower supplies and a glass of water. "Hello Grace," he says warmly.

"I've just had the pleasure of meeting your friend," Grace replies.

"My name's Amy," I say. "It has been really nice meeting you."

"Amy. What a beautiful name. You kids have fun, and mind your manners young man!" she says wagging her finger at Patrick.

"Scouts honor," Patrick flashes the boy-scout symbol and grins as we make our way from the table. "I brought you some water for taking your vitamins, and some bathing supplies for a shower," he says with satisfaction.

"My hero," I say popping the vitamins out of my bag. For some reason, I feel as though taking my vitamins makes everything okay. I'm in a strange place that no one else can see, having been chased and almost kidnapped by bad guys on the way here, but at least I've got my amino acids.

"The supplies are from my mom," he says leaning into the back of the door to the restroom. "The girl's showers are to the left."

I wind my way through stucco walls that curve to reveal four shower rooms, each with a white, almost translucent curtain. I take the one closest to the door and happily throw off the clothes covered in pins of horsehair. The shower water, nearly scalding hot, runs down my back, as my muscles relax into a deep blur of warmth. I rub the dust out of my eyes and start singing softly, "Day – o, me say da ay ay – o, Daylight come and me want to go home." The melody pours out of my vocal chords, elevating my mood. Suds pile up in my hair and I start swaying to the song in my head. "It's six-foot, seven-foot, eight-foot bunch! Daylight come and me and want to go home— "

I stop short as I hear another voice echo through the window above the shower, "and I wanna go home. Work all night, on a drink of rum." It's Patrick singing.

In a split second I'm confronted with a flurry of emotions. Slight panic gives way to the sound of his voice, and I decide to sing along. "Daylight come and me wanna go home." We both belt-out our best rendition of my favorite shower-time melody like no one's listening. "Stack banana till the morning come! Daylight come and me wanna go home." The echo rings throughout the entire bathroom and I'm pretty sure anyone in a five-mile radius can hear us. "Come mister tally man, tally me bananas…" I hear the sound of his voice trailing off as we slow down to end the song, "Daylight come and me wanna go home." I sense a small volcano of pleasure mounting in my chest, and barely manage to contain the grin erupting across my face. Rinsing the remaining suds out of my hair, I feel like I've been to confession and shared some secret part of myself as I step out of the shower and reach for the change of clothes in my bag. After washing the dirty laundry in the sink, I head out to look for Patrick. It doesn't take me long to find him waiting for me outside the bathroom.

"Feel better?" he asks.

"Yes, so much better," I say wringing the excess water out of my hair.

"I signed us up for dinner tomorrow night. We're making the speghetti," Patrick says in an Italian accent. "Porto vini, and Bottecelli, with a macaroni," he continues. It's hard not to laugh at his antics. He straightens up and his eyes narrow as if he is trying to figure me out. "I think we should go play. We have an hour before dinner, and there's some stuff I want to show you. He takes my hand and we walk back through the door to where the Tree of Life sways in the light of the giant glass dome ceiling. I can hear birds chirping and the leaves' reflection from the glass makes the entire room feel alive. We walk carefully over the roots and make our way to a clearing of rocks embedded in the soft earth.

"Isn't she magnificent?" he asks, slowly running his hand across the bark of a wondering branch. "When I was a kid I used to climb her and hide from everyone. Some of the monk's apprentices didn't think it was kosher, and I can still remember their faces trying to coax me to get down."

"It sounds like you had a pretty simple childhood," I say. "It also sounds like you were quite the handful."

"There will be hell to pay, I'm sure." He smiles and leans against the tree trunk. "Don't get me wrong, I love this tree completely – I always have. This is where I had my first experience with real meditation."

Patrick sits quietly at the base of the tree, and I cross my legs to sit beside him, resting my hands in the dirt behind me. I can feel the pulse of the tree emanating from the ground below and a steady stream of energy vibrating from the ground. The air feels slightly electric as I gaze up at the shadows of hundreds of branches. My perception shifts and I begin to see a soft haze of light surround the tree. The image of the tree fades and the soft light surrounding it intensifies to flashes of green and pink. I suddenly realize that we are connected, and the breeze passing through the leaves is the same breeze I feel in my heart. Everything seems softer, more translucent, and I lay on my back to take it all in. I've never felt such warmth, and I want to melt into the earth below. My fingers run through the dirt like travelers in a new world; they stumble upon a small rock and I sit up to examine it.

"It is all alive," I say smiling in wonderment. I focus on the rock and sense its vibration getting lighter, more elastic. Suddenly it floats out of my hand and hovers in the air. Patrick intently gazes upon it. The tiny piece of mineral slowly starts to spin in midair. I can see Patrick's eyes fixated through my own slightly blurred vision, and I realize I am freeing the rock, but he is the one making it spin. It comes to a stop and slowly falls back into my palm.

Several moments pass as we sit and adjust to what just happened. I've never seen anything like this before, and I can feel my entire world-view shift as I let it sink in. Patrick looks at me with disbelief. "So that's a new one," he says awkwardly, trying to find the right words. "Have you ever done that before?"

I laugh returning an equally surprised tone, "Uh, no."

"That was so fun," he says. He is grinning like a two year old who just got thrown up in the air for the first time. His eyes widen, "we should do that again."

"I don't know if I can," I say looking up at the tree and seeing a solid outline clearly contrasted from the light of the sun. "It just ... happened. I can't control it."

"What did it feel like?" he asks pulling me up with him.

"It felt kind of like with the purple flowers, but more conscious, more aware. I knew the tree differently."

"Could you tell the difference between yourself and the tree?" he asks.

"No. We were the same." I say clearly. "I know that sounds strange."

"No, no," he says shaking his head. "It's perfectly sane."

"I said 'strange.'" I correct him, a little unnerved by the implication that I might be going crazy.

"Amy, don't take this the wrong way. I think it's perfectly natural to feel at one with the tree. I know it can be a little scary opening yourself up like that."

"So you feel like this all of the time?" I ask leaning against the thick bark.

"No, not like this," he says. The words are forced, as if he is trying to speak for the first time. "Something tremendous has happened between us. I don't know how. Can you feel it?" He looks at me expectantly.

I know what he means. There is a clear spiral of energy running like the English Channel between us. I'm just too chicken to admit it. "What do you mean?" I ask innocently.

His eyes lower and he steps back slightly. "I don't know. It was just a feeling," he says shaking his head. "We should get going. They've already started with dinner."

We spoon piles of beans and rice over tortillas, and meander through the tables looking for Ana. Patrick is quiet, and I can tell he is brooding. Not seeing Ana anywhere, we settle on an empty table in the middle of the room. I feel like a tourist who missed the plane and now I'm left stranded with a pile of beans watching it take off into the sky. Why couldn't I just admit that I felt something? Would it be so bad? What was I afraid of? I push a single bean and corral it into the stacks of rice on my plate. Ana sits down at the table, almost without me noticing.

"How's it going?" she asks.

"Fine," Patrick replies mechanically.

"How was the afternoon?" Ana asks. "What did you guys do? Did you show Amy the music room? I hear Remi is going to host a jam after dinner."

"That sounds cool," Patrick says taking his first bite of food.

"Do you like music?" Ana asks me sincerely. Her green eyes are animated with dark curls of hair spiraling around them.

"I do," I reply. "I actually love music."

"I made Patrick take lessons until he was thirteen," she says ruffling his hair. "He hated the lessons, but you like to play now don't you honey? Remi!" Ana turns to greet a tall man with a long dark beard.

"May I join you?" he asks with a gentle voice. He is wearing a white linen shirt and sweat pants, and his eyes have a soft twinkle to them.

"Yes, please," Ana responds.

"It is fun to sit with the little songbirds I heard – there was beautiful singing in the hall earlier. Do you sing often?"

My eye-brows lift to apologize, as the words stumble out of my mouth, "No, not often."

"Well, it is nice to have some young people around here. Perhaps you can shake it up, bust some moves, so to speak, with the beats tonight.

Patrick can't help laughing, "That's right, Remi. There will be some moves to be busted. We'll take those beats out for dinner and a show, and then bring them back home before curfew."

"Somehow I don't remember you ever making curfew," Remi teases playfully.

"It sounds like Patrick was always in some kind of trouble," I comment.

"I remember this little tiger leaping out of the cabinet, scaring the gibbers out of me." Remi replies.

"You always fell for it," Patrick counters.

"I loved seeing your little face light up – so pleased you scared old Remi again."

"Let's just say, I never worried about Patrick not doing exactly what he wanted in life," Ana says. "It never seemed to matter to him how many times I asked him to wear a helmet, or put on a jacket, he always did exactly as he pleased."

Patrick shrugs his shoulders, "Ah, mom. You know I love you for trying. It couldn't have been easy raising such a miscreant," he jokes.

Remi turns to me, "I'm surprised you don't sing more often. You have perfect pitch. Do you play any instruments?"

"I learned to play the piano growing up, but I haven't played in years. I never liked having to read music," I say.

"I'm sure we can find a suitable instrument for you to jam on tonight. Or perhaps you will be inclined to sing a melody or two?" Remi winks.

I try to picture myself singing for a group of people I don't know. "I don't think so, but thanks for the offer," I say quickly.

"Well, come and hang out. It is good for the soul to how do you say, shake the booty?" Remi stands up and excuses himself from the table.

"He seems really nice," I say.

"Remi? He's the best," Patrick replies. "We've known him my whole life."

"I'm feeling tired. I think I will turn in early tonight. You guys go and have fun though," Ana says with a yawn. She stands up and squeezes Patrick's shoulder. "Goodnight sweetie pumpkin."

"Night mom," Patrick says softly.

"It is so nice to meet you," she says warmly to me. "See you guys in the morning."

"Sleep well," I say with a smile and a yawn.

"Oh no, you're not getting tired," Patrick commands. "Remi's jams are mind-blowing. You have to come."

"Okay, okay. I'm in," I say giving up on the idea of sleep.

We clean our dishes and head past what looks like an indoor green-house to the third wooden door on the right. "You are going to love this room," Patrick says excitedly. The door opens to reveal another stucco dome. Smooth chalk-white walls stream into a curved bench encircling the room. A line of instruments fill a crescent of the space, where Remi and some other musicians are tuning their instruments. I look up expecting to be amazed, and am still surprised by the ceiling. Hundreds of windows fill the dome with what appear to be crystals. "You should see it in the daylight – there are rainbows everywhere," Patrick explains.

"Little songbirds! I'm so happy you came! Come, make some harmonies with us!" Remi shouts across the dome.

We make our way across the wooden floor. "The acoustics vibrate everything in the room," Patrick explains. "My mom used to bring me here when I was sick, and after feeling the vibes from the music, I always got better." Besides Remi, there are five musicians standing in the pool of instruments. "Amy, this is Pedro, Conchita, Bailey, Erin, and Amen," Patrick introduces everyone. Each one acknowledges me with a nod and a warm smile. I nod in return and sense a rhythm flowing between them from their motions.

Remi sits on the floor tuning a very long-necked stringed instrument. "Please feel free to play with us," he says.

"Is that ... a sitar?" I ask excitedly.

"Yes, it has been in my family for generations," Remi replies.

I scan the sea of string, wood, metal and hide. I decide on a small drum.

"Tabla drums, nice choice," Patrick says laying his hands on the neck of a cello.

Remi closes his eyes and strums; a deep droning sound leads into a playful melody as his fingers bounce easily across six strings. Pedro caresses the guitar strings, while Bailey answers Remi's melody breathing through the wooden pipe of a flute. Erin holds another tabla drum and Conchita is dancing with her eyes closed to the sound of Amen strumming the thick strings of a base. I close my own eyes and hear Patrick enter the conversation with the low, ethereal voice of the cello. I can feel the pulse of sound overlap the drone of the sitar creating a release in my chest as I tap out a walking beat on the drum.

As we play, I begin to see the form of the music take shape in an image of lines interlacing each other. Conchita's voice carries a low and sultry sound throughout the room – almost like a gospel choir. Somehow her voice makes me feel safe, and my own melody joins Conchita's to lay out yet another layer of shapes interacting into a perfectly balanced whole. I feel the vibrations streaming through the openness in my chest and let my heart flow into the song. I open my eyes to see the room darkened, with silhouettes of human bodies oscillating throughout the room. I close them to enter back into the song and time seems to flow more slowly. We take the song and transform it several times, shaping it anew, but always keeping the original lyrical strain. When one player moves the beat, the others follow, as if we are all one organism.

When we stop, I open my eyes as if in a dream and see the others smiling back at me, cleansed. The crowd has dissipated, and I hug each of the other musicians before following Patrick back to the living space. We walk in silence, still feeling the hum of the music, to the cluster of paper walls, which reveal dozens of tiny bedrooms. Patrick leads me to a single bed, and I gratefully grasp the clean white sheets and fall into a deep sleep.

Chapter 8

I awake to a thin veil of warm sunlight pouring across the bed. It takes me a few minutes to realize where I am. My senses lull into focus on the white paper walls, the stucco windowsill, the meditation pillow sitting neatly in the center of the room, and the sound of human footsteps shuffling across the concrete floor. Oh yea, I'm at an invisible spiritual retreat center in the middle of New Mexico, aka Entael.

I sit up to the sound of Patrick's voice, and realize I slept in my jeans and t-shirt. I can feel the memory of singing my heart out last night as a warm buzz. That was real, I think to myself; I didn't just dream it.

"Good morning sunshine," Patrick's voice radiates through the paper wall. "Are you decent?"

"Yea, come on in," I manage.

"I thought we could start out the morning with a little yoga – what do you think?" he asks enthusiastically.

"Really? Yoga. Right now," I respond squinting to see him through the sunlight.

"Heck yea! This is the best time for it – your mind is still partially asleep so your body can do its thing without all the yammering of your thoughts. It'll be great, I promise," he assures me. Once again, I find myself being compelled into some strange new activity by Patrick. What is it about him that does this to me? His smile perhaps? Am I getting somehow hypnotized by the brazen look in his eyes? Whatever it is, something about how he moves makes me want to jump in to the deep end of any pool. I'm really going to have to start paying attention to his powers of persuasion – especially if I expect to sleep-in anytime soon. "I brought you some yoga pants from my mom," he says.

"Great," I say with feigned enthusiasm. He saunters behind the paper wall, while I slip on the stretchy tie-dyed tights. It is up for debate on whether or not I am a fool, but I certainly look like one. "Okay, let's do this," I say stepping out into the line of public sight.

Patrick leads us to the first door on the left of the living quarters into yet another dome. There is a line of windows spanning the circumference of the room. At the top of the ceiling, tiny balls of grey and white form what appears to be a sort of yin and yang symbol spiraling around each other and outward to cover the entire dome. I have the feeling I'm staring up at a galaxy of stars swirling through the expanse of the universe.

"Wow," I say catching my breath.

"This is the universal harmony room," Patrick explains. "People come here to find balance, which explains the yoga," he says smiling. I look around to see the contours of several human bodies in what seem to be impossible postures throughout the room.

"Okay, let's do this. Where are the mats?" I ask.

"We don't need mats – it's way better without the mats," he replies. I run the ball of my foot across the dark blue stone floor. I'm a little taken aback; having done yoga a few times in the past with my mom, we always had mats. "Okay, so feel free to do whatever feels right to you. I'm just going to lead us through some initial stuff," he says. He stretches his arms out with his hands pointed upright, and then proceeds to lean over and press his hands on the floor. I follow along. "Don't forget to breath," he says pushing back. My hamstrings are burning, as I look up to see the white beard of the older Indian man I remember from lunch yesterday.

"Hello," he says with the same twinkle flashing in his eyes. Wiry, ropes of white hair sprout like firecrackers from his brow-line. "I couldn't help but notice you stretching the Svanasana in a way that will only cause frustration. Try to push more from the pinkies of your fingers." As I press through my pinky fingers, my entire back shifts back. "There, that is better yes?" he asks with a kindness I have never felt from any teacher ever. "You are friends practicing together yes?" he asks.

"Yea," I say straining to breathe while looking up.

"I see," he says knowingly. "Will you take some advice from old Rajib on this fine morning?"

"Yes please," I say quickly. Judging from his knowledge of the pinky fingers, I'm pretty sure I, at least, could use his help.

Patrick stands upright and bows with his hands pressed together. I quickly follow suit, managing to copy his gestures and lower my head just as Patrick raises his.

"We would be honored. Rajib, this is Amy. Amy, this is Rajib, a great teacher," Patrick says reverently. I look up to see Rajib's eyes sparkling with the innocence of a small child.

"Let's start with Virabhadrasansa," he says gracefully moving one leg straight back and leaning forward like superman. The weight of his rather large belly doesn't seem to slow him down, and with exception of his right leg running straight to the floor, he looks like a swimmer in midair. Patrick and I do our best to imitate his posture. "Now change," Rajib steps down and assumes the posture with his left leg rising from the floor. He rations quick orders, "Keep your hips level, your gaze soft. Pull your knee caps up. Focus on your breath – your breath is all you are." Next, he has us hold wooden blocks between our thighs while keeping our hands clasped behind our backs. "It is time for Sarvangasana," he says while gracefully raising his legs up from his shoulders. I press my shoulders back onto a blanket and rest my head on the floor. I notice Patrick is pushing the weight of his body up into the air, and mimic his posture. "Breath here," Rajib suggests pressing into my diaphragm. His voice reminds me of a doctor, and I can tell he understands every part of the human body. We sit nearly upside-down for what feels like hours, when he finally has us lower our legs, grateful for the floor. "You are a couple yes?" Rajib asks.

"We're, um ... friends," Patrick stumbles to reply.

"Good. Friends can support each other in both the mind and the body," Rajib comments. "Patrick should take Sarvangasana once more, but this time keep your back on the floor so you can support Amy in her own pose."

"What?" I ask forgetting my filter. "I'm sorry, what pose?"

Rajib doesn't blink, and looks at me innocently as he says, "Don't worry, Patrick will provide a foundation for you to strengthen your back." He motions for me to stand facing away from Patrick's legs. "Amy, you bend back, letting Patrick hold your weight. Patrick, keep your toes on her lower lumbar, and reach up to hold her shoulders," Rajib instructs.

I just stand there for a moment, thinking about whether this is going to work. With all of the other poses, I was able to watch someone else doing it first, to know it was actually possible. With this one, I have to trust that it would work. Not to mention, having to lean my bottom back onto Patrick's feet – does Rajib even realize this is awkward? I know we are technically friends, but it still feels weird.

"Go ahead, don't be afraid. Patrick will hold you," Rajib coaxes. I step backwards enough to feel Patrick's legs on mine and lean back onto his feet. Panic starts to set in as I lift my own feet off the floor and roll my head backward to balance on his feet like a scale. My head teeters slightly and I start to pull upward until I feel Patrick's warm grasp on my shoulders. I breathe a sigh of relief and lean back to see Patrick's upside-down face gazing up at me.

"Don't worry, I've got you," he whispers with a smile.

"Very good," Rajib says. "It is good to trust one another. Now reach back and stretch to hold your ankles. Feel the pose and connect your gaze upon each other."

I take a deep constrained breath and focus my attention upon Patrick. I could fall at the slightest falter of his hold. He stars back unflinching. Strangely, I feel free, swinging upside-down and completely vulnerable, my eyes clear and unthinking. I feel a twang in my chest as if a flock of birds have broken free from wires I'd contrived to hold them back, and I stare back into his eyes, completely balanced, hanging from his feet.

"Amy, when you are ready, release your ankles and rise up. Patrick, slowly lower your feet to release her," Rajib instructs. I rise up slowly, acclimating to the flow of blood rushing to and from my head. I reach to place my feet back on the floor, and turn to Rajib's quiet and electric gaze. I feel a deep sense of appreciation for him, and bow instinctively. Rajib responds with a nod of his head and places his hands together in acknowledgment. "Namaste," he says turning to leave.

"Namaste," I reply still bowing. I'm not exactly sure what that word means, but it seems like a nice way to say thanks. With my hands pressed together and gazing down, I realize I am partially bowing to the feeling inside myself. This is the third time since coming here that I feel a strong but secret happiness bursting out uncontrollably. I smile to myself and then look up to see Patrick doing a hand stand.

"Are you ready for some breakfast?" he asks.

"So ready."

The living quarters are crowded, and nearly all of the tables are full as we carefully carry our bowls of steaming hot oatmeal to a table near back entrance. Ana joins us carrying a carafe of orange juice.

"How was the party?" she asks.

"Amy sang. It was awesome," Patrick brags.

Blushing slightly, I reply, "I had so much fun." I dig into my oatmeal and I've never tasted anything so good. There are strawberries and some kind of cream mixed into the steaming white oats. "What is in this stuff? It is the best thing ever."

"The food here has a higher vibration," Ana explains. "We've done tests, and you can actually photograph the light radiating from the food at Entail. You can also raise the vibration of food outside of Entael, and we've documented this with multiple tests." Ana holds her bowl of oats gently in her palms and closes her eyes. "Sometimes I picture the highest form of light radiating from my hands, and when I'm not staying here, I actually picture being here, and have had success with that as well."

"Mom, stop. Please. You are going to freak her out," Patrick pleads.

"No, really – I don't mind. This is fascinating," I say holding Patrick's arm.

"If you are really interested you should stop by the meditation chambers after breakfast. I would be happy to show you what we've been working with," Ana says.

"Only if you really want to," Patrick cautions.

"I want to," I say emphatically. I don't know what Patrick is trying to protect me from, but his mom is anything but boring – maybe a little kooky, but definitely not boring.

As we clean off our bowls and I resist the temptation to go in for more. We walk through the Tree of Life dome to the second door on the left of the stained glass room into a new dome. Inside, the roof is completely made of wood, with concentric circles lining the ceiling like latitudinal lines on a topographical map of the world. The floor is concrete, with thick inlaid lines filled with what looks like sand. There are several meditation stools, mats, pillows and trays scattered in various spaces around the room; a few participants are seated with their eyes closed. The faint smell of sage and cedar envelop the room, and for the first time since I've been here I feel like I'm in a desert. Ana leads us to a tray near the entrance and pulls up three meditation pillows to sit on. On the tray there are thousands of tiny pieces of what look like broken mechanical pencil lead.

"It all started when I was working in the field. I found that my very presence would influence the results of the molecular reactions. Then we realized that the molecules acted like waves at times, and finally figured out that if we saw them as waves, then they behaved like waves – which meant everything could be perceived as vibration. Our entire theory of molecular processes could be replaced with a more refined, more accurate model of vibration. What we discovered was that consciousness also operated vibrationally, so your thoughts influence –subtly at times, the world around you. Once we started acknowledging this, the effects grew stronger. Pretty soon, government agencies were wanting to know what we were up to, and the Valencia wanted to control our every move. We were guided to find this place, and have continued to work here in secrecy ever since." I sit on the pillow digesting every word. I'd almost forgotten about the Valencia, and why everything must be kept a secret.

"These are just broken pieces of lead," Ana continues. "Through the years, various practitioners have been able to align all of the pieces to face one direction. Go ahead, Patrick, show her how this happens."

Patrick rolls his eyes, "Okay mom," he says reluctantly. How many times has he been in here practicing with these things? And I thought ballet lessons were rough. He focuses his gaze upon the tray of lead pieces and at first nothing happens. I start to get a little worried that he might not be able to perform on cue, when one solo piece of lead twitches. Soon dozens follow, until the entire tray is filled will thousands of tiny sticks all aligned in the exact same direction. Patrick raises his eye-brow, struts his finger in our direction, and says sarcastically, "And the show will be here all week so don't miss the next exciting performance."

"That was amazing," I counter.

He shakes his head. "That was nothing. I am only capable of aligning and ordering less organized matter – you have something completely different. You can slow down time."

I shake my head trying to retract his words. "I don't know about that."

"Yes, you do. You get this look in your eyes, and then you move lightning fast. I've seen it."

"Is this true?" Ana asks me with a tone of seriousness I haven't heard her take before.

"I guess so," I reply. "It happens when I focus on tiny details. And then sometimes I feel solid objects get really light and buzzing – vibrating."

"It's true mom, just trust us on this one," Patrick comments.

Ana is already up on her feet and retrieving what looks like an old nautical sand timer – with glass cups on either end and one side heavy with small grains of sand. "Let's try it," she says enthusiastically. I look around to see there is still one person sitting upright on the far right side of the room.

"I don't want to disturb any..."

"You won't," Ana replies. "Everyone is used to this space being a room for playing with consciousness. See how long it takes you to retrieve the hat left across the room." Ana excitedly holds the timer with a look of anticipation.

"Okay. I'll try," I say. "Just give me a minute to focus." I take a deep breath and try to slow down my thoughts. I glance over at Patrick, and I notice the length of one of his eye-lashes as he blinks. I stand up, and see Ana slowly turning over the timer. The tiny grains of sand fall like snowflakes, and I turn my gaze to the hot pink hat on the floor. I effortlessly move my legs, bounding like a gazelle across the room to retrieve the hat, and do a double-take as my hand seems translucent – I can almost see through it. I refocus, and I'm back before the first grain of sand touches the glass. Ana pushes the timer over. She looks stunned.

"My turn," Patrick says. I can tell this is driving the competitive part of him a little crazy. He stands up and sprints across the room, touches the wall and sprints back.

Still wide-eyed, Ana works to regain her composure. "That was about 4 seconds," she reports.

"That has to be about 15 yards," Patrick says.

"You did great honey," Ana comforts. "But I'm afraid Amy somehow beat you by nearly all 4 seconds." She turns to face me, "Amy, that was unbelievable. How did you do that?"

"I don't know. Tiny details become clearer, and pretty soon everything is moving really slow – except me."

"We have had people levitating their own bodies before. Bosho talked about it as being able to accept all things as they are – pure light. This, he claimed, brought the awareness of connection, and a feeling of expansion beyond himself. Does this sound familiar?" Ana asks.

"Actually, yes. That's exactly what it feels like. It's like I'm expanding my perception to take it all in, and when I do this, it becomes more fluid – easier to move through."

"Yes, yes. This means our consciousness not only directly orders matter, but can actually reposition its relation so that everything becomes more malleable – fascinating," Ana exclaims. Her smile fades and her tone becomes serious, "it also means you are a prime target for the Valencia. It is better they not know you can do this, and I strongly recommend that you not practice this in public. We don't want them tracking you."

"Okay," I say nodding my head. It's not like I plan on giving out free shows or joining the Olympics anytime soon.

"And that means you too mister," she tells Patrick. "Until I know what Luca wants its better to play it safe. Parker should be here tomorrow so we should know more then."

"Who is Parker?" I ask.

"Parker is a very gifted psychic. He can view any place you want – remotely," Patrick answers. "He's also 100% flaming gay," Patrick adds with a smile, "He's a great guy."

I'm beginning to wrap my brain around what this all means. I have a tendency to reposition matter, which I need to keep secret from the Valencia, a group of tools we are going to spy on with the help of Patrick's psychic friend. As we walk back to the living quarters to eat some "vibrationally enhanced" vegetarian food, I pinch myself to make sure I'm not dreaming.

Chapter 9

I smile to see Pedro and Conchita having lunch at a table by the windows. I carefully balance a bowl full of edamame pods with a hot cup of tea and approach their table.

"Conchita right?" I ask.

"Yes, but you can call me Chita," she says flirtatiously. I sit down next to her. "That was wonderful singing with you last night," she says. Her voice is rich and sultry like a 1920's actress, and her eyes glitter with enjoyment. I notice Pedro smile and nod, looking affectionately at her.

"It was a very fun night," he adds. I catch myself staring at the length of Pedro's eyelashes. I've never seen eyelashes so lush; his eyes have a kind of sweetness to them – the kind I've seen before in the eyes of babies first learning how to walk.

"It was – you were amazing," I say taking a sip of tea.

Patrick makes his way to a seat next to Pedro. "Hey man," he says warmly. "It's good to see you guys. How long are you here?"

"Just until tomorrow," Chita says. "We have a gig in San Diego. Are you staying long? Visiting your mama?"

Patrick looks at me, unsure of what to say. "I think we are staying for the week," he says hesitantly.

"This place is amazing," I reply.

"It is funny how we never stay long, but when we are away we always think about coming back," Chita says laughing. "It must have been quiet a trip to grow up here."

"Somehow it doesn't seem weird to me – just hard to avoid getting in trouble with so many adults. My mom had a hive of baby-sitters, and apparently she needed them." Patrick's mouth extends into an especially mischievous grin. "It was a little strange visiting my dad in a world with so much plastic and commercials. I remember staring at the commercials – like why are all the ladies acting like that?"

"I know right?" Chita nods. "So crazy…"

"So you were home-schooled?" I ask.

"Yea, except for a couple of years when I lived with my dad, and since my sophomore year in high-school," Patrick replies. "It was me and whatever book my mom had assigned, and of course there were plenty of spiritual masters to keep me in line."

"It must have been so tight learning how to play with Remi," Pedro comments. "I adore that man."

"Yea, you do. You would probably save the sweat from his jams in a jar if you could," Chita teases.

"Maybe I will…" Pedro threatens half joking.

"Don't get me wrong, I love Remi too, but just not as much as Pedro. Hey, what are you guys doing this afternoon? We were going to go for a hike if you want to come," Chita almost sings the offer.

I look at my phone and realize that I should probably call my mom. "I can't. But I'll walk up with you on the way to make some phone calls," I reply. I tuck my phone snuggly in my back pocket and we head to the kitchen to wash our dishes. Patrick pulls me aside with a serious look on his face.

"Amy, I know it's really hard, but you have to keep the heavy-duty details on the down-low. You can't tell anyone about Entael – not yet. When we bring people into the fold, we trust them to keep it a secret.

"Do you really need to remind me? I got it Patrick. I can't tell anyone. It's not that I am going to – I just hate lying."

"I'm sorry," he says. "You're right. I don't mean to be a dick. I feel overprotective of the situation for some reason. I don't know. It's not usually my thing. Listen, is there anything I can do to help? Do you want me to talk to your friend?"

I think about this for a minute. Patrick has a way of influencing people, and it would be nice for Ally to get to know him just a little. "Okay, I say. Talk to Ally. That would be great."

We meet Pedro and Chita at the door and head up the hill to find service. The sky is completely clear and the sun beams down making the landscape glow. I can't tell if it's just my imagination, but the plants look brighter, somehow more alive. I've been here for less than two days, and already Entael seems to have affected my perception. Chita and Pedro hold hands as they trek up the path, and even when they walk it seems more like their dancing. At the road we part ways with Pedro and Chita and I give Ally a call.

"Amy, hey – how's it going?" Ally sounds like she's waking up from a nap.

"It's going good. We are having a blast."

"Your mom called. I told her you were in the shower, and she seemed to buy it," Ally says dryly.

"I'm so sorry. Thank you for doing that. I promise I'm totally safe and Patrick is a really great guy and you are a great friend for covering for me," I say channeling a care-bear.

"Yea, yea. I'm so awesome. I know," she replies sarcastically. "Have you guys made out yet?"

"Ally! Shut up," I say turning away from Patrick's gaze. "You know I don't do that – way too awkward. That one time sophomore year doesn't count."

"Oh, you mean the slobber-fest behind the lockers with Jonathan Brody? That was an unfortunate event. Maybe you should just avoid contact with boys from now on."

"I've thought about that, but I think he's really a good person. You should say hi." I hand the phone to Patrick.

"What?" Ally demands.

"Hi, Ally," Patrick says. "I know you don't know me, and you have every reason to be skeptical, but I want you to know it's all good. We are just kicking it." I can vaguely hear the sound of Ally's voice coming out of the cell phone at Patrick's ear. "Okay, I got it. Loud and clear," Patrick says quickly. "I promise that won't be necessary... Yes. I understand." He hands me the phone looking like he's had his shirt handed to him.

"He actually sounds like a nice guy," Ally says cheerfully.

"What did you say to him?" I ask laughing.

"I just threatened to remove his testicles."

"Oh, that was nice. I'm glad you are off to a good start. Listen, I am losing service and I need to call me mom," I say.

"Okay, I love you. Be safe."

We hang up and I look at Patrick. For the first time he looks genuinely frightened. "I'm sorry," I say. "Ally can be a little blunt at times."

"She threatened ... to cut off my privates," Patrick stutters. "Who does that?"

"That just means she cares. She is really a sweetheart," I say.

"A regular Mother-Teresa," he comments sarcastically.

I phone my mom and step a few yards down the hill to sit on a rock, prepared for the lie-fest.

"Hello?"

"Hey mom."

"Honey how are you? I have been missing you. I called yesterday but Ally said you were in the shower. Why doesn't your phone pick up?" I can tell from her voice my mom is talking while driving.

"I miss you too. I'm good – just kicking it. My phone has been acting weird. I think we may need to replace it," I say.

"Yea, the signal is cutting out. Well, I'm glad you guys are having fun. I have to go. I'm in the car. Call me later in the week – maybe from Ally's phone."

"Okay mom," I sigh. "I love you."

"Love you too honey." She hangs up.

I stare out over the horizon and try to shake that numb feeling that comes over me when I lie. I wiggle my toes and stretch out onto the boulder. Patrick comes bounding down the hillside.

"How did it go?" he asks.

"It went okay," I reply.

"Can we go play now? I want to show you the music room while it's still light," Patrick says pouncing on the rock next to my boulder; he crouches on the rock pinching a blade of grass between his teeth. "Come on, Amy... you know you want to," he says tickling my face with the soft end of the blade.

"No, let's just lie here and sleep," I beg.

He pushes me gently at first and then starts to roll me off my boulder. I am shocked to feel myself fall off the rock and I barely land on feet. I feel a rush of anger and glimpse him galloping back down the hillside. "You're so dead!" I shout. My senses are alert, and I catch up to him easily, jumping onto his back to tackle him to the ground. We roll down the last few yards of hillside; the pain of the cuts and bruises is tempered by laughter. It feels good to pick on Patrick – safe somehow. I've never had a sibling, but I imagine this is what it feels like. We walk toward Entael covered in dust, feeling the aches of a few bruises but more alive because of them. I shake the powdery dirt off of my shirt and shove him back from the door one last time before entering Entael. We both head to the kitchen for water and after going to the bathroom to wash my face, Patrick leads me excitedly to the music room.

"You've got to see the rainbows," he urges me through the door. The room is empty with the exception of hundreds of palm-sized rainbows scattered across the floor and the line of instruments to the left. The light is unbearably beautiful and a soft haze permeates the air. "The light vibrates," Patrick comments, "when we play you can almost see it." I walk over to the row of instruments, my eye on the cello.

"I've always wanted to play this," I comment.

"Try it out," Patrick offers. He pulls up a large wooden chair with long spindles running down the back. I sit down and gingerly place the curved shape between my legs. "Take the bow in your right hand, like this," he instructs grasping his hand over my own, and gently pushing my thumb down to pull the bowed hair across the metal strings. A sound erupts and echoes throughout the room; the light does in fact appear to vibrate, and the entire room buzzes from the echo. I look up at him and smile. "Yes, that's good," he replies. "Now, take your left hand and place your fingers on the strings like this," he says swinging his leg through to sit directly behind me.

My heart races slightly, and I take a deep breath trying to focus on getting my fingers to firmly hold down the metallic wire. His chest presses slightly upon my shoulder blades, and I can feel the gentle rhythm of his breathe on my neck. His hand guides my fingers to coerce the bow, until the strings vibrate in undulating waves. Our breathing matches the rhythm of the sound and I start to experiment with a small melody, vaguely resembling an Irish hymn. The sound opens my heart, and I can feel a channel of what seems to be golden energy linking us, pouring out of our chests. I can sense his left hand drift off of the neck of instrument and make its way to my waist. I continue the melody, and the pattern speeds up, shifting, slightly off-kilter. I turn to feel his jaw sweeping my shoulder and whisper in my ear, "Tell me you can't feel this."

I turn my eyes to meet his, "I can feel it," I confirm kissing him squarely on the mouth. I kiss him easily, as if I've done this a thousand times before. We drop the bow, and I can feel his left hand wind its way across my stomach and past my ribs to graze the curve of my breast. An alarm begins to sound inside and I almost pull back before I feel his hand gently press against the center of my chest. He is feeling the energy pouring from my heart. I turn completely around to face him and the pulse of emotion is completely unleashed; we rush to kiss every part of each other. My lips graze his ear, and his mouth opens to caress my jaw. I can feel the flutter of his eyelash on my neck, and the soft scratch of his chin on my cheek. We are like homing birds, finally finding each other, coming home.

I can't satiate my craving to touch him, to kiss every part of him. I straddle his legs on the chair and begin to unbutton his shirt, kissing a path down his chest. He leans back and the chair tips; I place my feet on the floor to hold us upright, and press my hand down on his chest, looking deep into the green irises staring up at me. "What time is it?" I ask as I notice the light in the rainbows fading with the sun.

"Oh crap," he says sitting up. "We are in charge of dinner." I start laughing because somehow that seems hilarious right now. He buttons his shirt and I return the cello back to its stand. We walk out of the music room trying to order ourselves, while simultaneously stealing kisses, with guilty expressions on our faces. It feels like we've broken more than a few rules, although I can't really think what they are.

On the way to the kitchen, we pass through the greenhouse. Everything is white. Bright light pours through white coverings over hundreds of luscious green plants. "It's hydroponic," Patrick explains. "They grow better this way." The warm humid air fills my lungs, and I notice there isn't any dirt holding the roots, just water. Patrick collects some basil and oregano leaves and has me carry several heads of lettuce and a lemon. With our booty in hand we head to the kitchen. The cement floor of the kitchen area is a painted chessboard, with a large wooden cutting table in the center of the room. A wide and deep stainless-steal sink sits next to an old shelving unit filled with containers of dried spices, berries, oats, and canned goods. Patrick reaches for a huge pot and begins to fill it with water. He lifts it to the stove, and lights a bloom of flame underneath.

"Cooking for so many people must be a challenge yes?" I ask.

"I guess so. It seems normal to me," he says towel-drying the lettuce. "When I cook at my dad's, it seems like such a waste to only feed two people. And this way, we get to enjoy all kinds of different stuff." He stops and looks at me seriously. "Have you ever tried a fresh tomato?"

"No, but I've had lots of tomatoes..."

"You gotta try one," he says biting into the bright red roundness. I look at him with skepticism and take a bite. The sweetness surprises me.

"This is really good," I say with a smile. The juice erupts from the fruit and he leans in to wipe the dripping sweetness from my chin.

"Do you want to chop some herbs with me?" He says with some swagger reaching back to turn on a small transistor radio; the sound of Etta James flows into the air. I take a small knife and slice through a pile of oregano. Patrick sings along with Etta as he unloads the tomatoes onto the stove. I can feel his hips rocking to the music behind me and I start to sway to the hopeful rhythm. I feel his lips graze my neck, and pretty soon we are lost in the charm of each other's eyes, swaying to the beat. We don't even notice the water boiling-over on the stove until bubbles of steam burst like a dragon coughing behind us.

"Whoa! Hold on there," Patrick drags the loaded pot off of the flame. "We better focus on dinner," he says laughing. We spend the rest of the time like good little cooks, and serve the piping hot pasta only seven minutes late.

After dinner, while Patrick is chatting with his mom, Remi, Chita and Pedro, I sneak off to lay on the futon bedding and be alone. I stare up at the circling lines on the curved ceiling and hear the faint echo of their conversations. My pulse slows and I feel the rise and fall of my breath with my hand resting on my diaphragm. The curved lines dance into a moving image in my unconscious and become my last thought before sleep.

Chapter 10

I wake to the sensation of Patrick lying next to me, playing with a strand of my hair. Rays of sunlight stream across the room, and I can see particles of dust floating in the light, like tiny planets dangling in space. Patrick smells like a combination cedar and sage, and I lean in to inhale the aroma from his neck.

"Did you sleep here?" I ask.

"No, I've just been watching you sleep since the sun came up," he replies stroking my bangs. "Is that okay?"

I pause to contemplate this. What is it like to watch me sleep? Do I snore? I am not responsible for my actions when I'm dreaming, and I wonder if I talk in my sleep. On the other hand, his tone is full of adoration, and maybe it's not so bad having a sleep watcher. He rolls his leg on top of my thigh and the sheets bundle and spill out of the gap between our legs. "Yea, it's okay," I say warmly looking into his eyes. "It's just that I've never had a boyfriend before, so it's just different I guess."

He nods his head and suddenly looks like he has someplace to be. "Can we not use labels for what we have going here?" he asks.

"What do you mean?" I say sitting up.

"Can I just be Patrick, and I don't want you to be my "girlfriend" – I want you to be you. Amy. I just think all the labels end up screwing with everything.

"So, we're not going out?" I ask pulling my leg from under his.

"Whoa, slow down. I didn't mean that," he says reaching for my waist. "I just think what we have is really special, and I want to let it breathe and grow on its own. I think I'm falling pretty hard for you Amy. I just want to ride this out without the weight of pre-determined expectations on us. Is that okay?"

Really? I think to myself. The first time I feel something like this for someone and we can't even say we're sort of a couple? "I feel like if I can't call it something then it's not as real," I say.

He gently tugs on the sheet looking down. "No, Amy. It's more real. It gets to live," he says.

"So our relationship is a living creature?" I ask deviously.

"I guess you could call it that," he says with a smile.

"Alright, I'm happy to be having a living creature with you," I say. I pause to reconsider. "That just sounds bad."

"Scandalous," he says laughing. "I'm happy to be in a living creature with you," he tries.

"Okay, I'll take it," I reply. "It won't make sense to anyone else, but I guess that doesn't really matter."

"No, it doesn't," he says kissing me on the lips. Our fingers run through one another's hair as we stare into each other's eyes, almost forgetting where we are. I can feel the pulse of energy connecting between us, in a translucent light with hints of pink. The footsteps in the commons area multiply and slowly the hum of conversations steals our attention. The sound of our stomach's growling like pterodactyls talking finally pulls us out of the bed.

There is left-over oatmeal and granola for breakfast. We sit down next to Ana. The usual orange juice carafe is half full. She sits huddled over a piece of paper and her tea, scribbling notes.

"Hey guys," she says distractedly.

"What you got there mom?" Patrick asks crunching into an apple.

"I'm working out a theory for Amy's influence on matter. Her attention shifts the vibration of her surroundings, making matter malleable – more susceptible to coding. The question is to what extent and in what ways is she affected by it?" She turns to look up at me. "You are able to move more quickly through the environment during this process. Do you notice any other effects?"

I look down at my palm and speak softly, "I could see through my hand yesterday. I don't know why, but it became translucent."

"Really?" Patrick asks with concern. "You didn't tell me that. What does that mean?"

"Did you feel scared?" Ana asks me.

"No, actually, I felt really calm."

"I wouldn't worry too much – yet. Later, I would like to run some tests if that's okay with you."

"Sure," I say.

She gazes over my shoulder to the entrance. I turn to see two figures cross the room carrying duffel bags. "Parker!" Ana gets up to greet him with a hug. His smile is contagious, and almost distracts from his attire; with a denim shirt unbuttoned halfway down his chest, he is wearing linen pants that are tight-rolled as if he just stepped out of a scene from back to the future, revealing bare ankles cradled in extra-plush moccasins. His eyes are shaded by bright pink sunglass lenses.

"Ana, my darling. How are you?" he asks enthusiastically, releasing his bear-hug.

"Good, it's been good," she explains. "Who is your friend?"

"This is Gavin. I met him back east at a thing." Parker says cheerfully. Gavin also stands out in nearly all black clothing with a studded black leather jacket. I catch myself staring at his eyes – they seem to burn with flames of amber, and it feels like I've seen them before but I can't remember where.

"Pleased to meet you," Gavin motions to shake Ana's hand while looking at me.

"This is my son Patrick, and his friend Amy," Ana introduces us.

"Hey man," Patrick says shaking Gavin's hand and working to get his attention.

"Hi," I say with a small wave averting my eyes. Lending a distraction from the awkwardness of the introduction, Ana offers to take Parker and Gavin to their living spaces.

Just when they are out of range, Patrick turns around in a flurry, his arms flailing. "What the hell is he thinking? Bringing a stranger he's just met to Entael. This is not cool," Patrick fumes.

"Couldn't he say the same thing about you?" I tease.

"That's totally different," Patrick counters. "I know you."

"There was something different about his eyes," I say.

"Yea, they couldn't stop staring at you."

"Are you jealous?" I ask playfully and push on his shoulder, throwing him off-balance.

"Me? No –," he says emphatically. "I just don't like him. I can't read him."

Parker saunters back over to us. I notice he's wearing gold bracelets and he could definitely use a shave. "How's my favorite yardbird?" he asks patting Patrick on the back.

"Hey, man. It's good to see you," Patrick says shaking his hand. "Who is this guy," he nods his head in the direction of the living spaces. "How do you know him?"

"He's just a friend – why is it that all of the really good looking ones have to be straight? I met him at a party in Boston. He's in grad school studying neurology." Parker's eyes open wide and he looks like a mad-scientist, squeezing his fingers on an imaginary cerebrum, "the study of the brain." His eyes are quick and shift easily as he talks without any indication of stopping. "Anyway, he's a perfect traveling companion, and he has an acute talent for keeping me on track – you know my attention tends to stray from any particular course. We had been all over Boston and New York, and he said he'd never been out west and so here we are."

"And you trust him?" Patrick asks incredulously.

"Patrick, please. Sweetie, I am psychic and I am an excellent judge of character. Anyway, he won't divulge anything – you will be lucky to get three words out of him. Now stop worrying. It doesn't suit you," he says turning his attention to me. "And how do you know the yard bird?"

"Patrick? Um, we met at school," I reply.

"Well, it's a pleasure to make your acquaintance. Amy is it?"

"Yes," I say shaking his hand. I see his eyes close behind the pink shades for a second and when he opens them he looks at me differently, as if he has had a revelation.

"I see," he says turning to Patrick. "You've brought yourself a little coder friend. You really do have a knack for finding treasure now don't you?"

"What do you mean – treasure?" I ask him slightly annoyed. Parker raises an eyebrow in surprise and pauses to contemplate my reaction.

"I didn't mean to offend you – you are developing an incredible gift, and it really is a pleasure to meet you." His words sound like a white flag and I relax the tension in my jaw. "It's just that Patrick is well practiced in the art of thievery."

Patrick grins at me, and I can see how he's gotten away with it – that smile is completely insurmountable. I swear it causes amnesia.

Ana's clogs tap loudly across the floor and her slender arms wrap around Patrick and Parker's shoulders. "I hate to bring up the issue, but the Valencia are after Patrick again, and we really need to see what they are up to."

"See what I mean? What have you stolen now?" Parker demands with a smile.

"I didn't steal anything. Mom returned the scroll, and they still came after us."

"Well, why don't we take a little peek at what the "secret" brotherhood is up to?" Parker asks playfully.

Ana leads us past the Tree of Life to a door on the right. The room is lit by a clear glass ceiling, and the light shines down in circular flower patterns that reflect upon the floor. "This is the language of light," Ana comments walking across the circular reflections. "It is the underlying code for all life." Once again, I am struck by the beauty of the space, and feel as though my cells are spinning to the patterns of light filling the room.

Parker sits cross-legged on a meditation pillow and closes his eyes. "Where do you want me to go?" he asks cheerfully.

"Please go where ever Luca Fieri is," Ana instructs.

Parker speaks as the images come to his mind. "I see a large castle – the Necoli Castle, in the great hall there are a number of men. They are all wearing masks, but I can see Luca. He is sitting at the head of the table. He is saying something about a scroll. He says the missing page of the Indus script must be found. The others are talking all at once, something about a plan – that the plan won't work. There is lots of banging on the table. They are arguing. Now the image is fading. I can't see anymore." Parker opens his eyes and looks at Patrick. "I thought you said you gave them the scroll."

Patrick looks guilty. "Most of it," he confesses.

"Patrick Michael Flynn! What do you mean 'most of it'?" Ana demands.

"All of it, except for one page. I didn't know what it meant at first, but I do now, and they can't have it."

"What are you talking about," Ana half cries in frustration. She is pacing back and forth.

"Okay. You know how I can code a structure of tendencies that people can temporarily fall into if their consciousness is less ordered at the time?"

We all nod. Apparently Patrick has been influencing people for a while.

"The Indus script allows us to communicate telepathically, without words. But there is a way it can translate directly into your thoughts – to where you think you are the one responsible for the thought. It would make it possible for them to manipulate people's minds directly without any knowledge that these thoughts aren't really yours. It is like the atom bomb of mind control."

"Wait a minute. Don't they keep a copy of this scroll lying around somewhere?" I ask sarcastically.

"You need the original to decode it. You have to retrace how it was made exactly," Patrick replies. "I had sort of hoped they wouldn't notice – that somehow they didn't know what it meant. But apparently the douchebags are smarter than I thought."

"I can't believe this is happening." Ana says. She has her hands crossed on her chest and for the first time since I've known her I see a streak of fear in her eyes. "They won't stop until they have the missing page. You have to give it to them."

"Hold on Ana, maybe Patrick is right. If the Valencia have access to this page, it would expand their control over people. This could change history; this could be worse than television," Parker reasons.

All of this talk about the Valencia coming after us is making my skin crawl. I take out my vitamin container and pop some vitamin B.

"Mom, they can't have it. I think we should destroy it," Patrick argues.

"And what then? They will hunt you forever. I can't bear that," Ana cries.

Ana paces back and forth like a prisoner. Parker, on the other hand looks amused.

"Look, we don't fully understand this process. My sense is if we destroy it, we will lose important insight into things we don't even understand yet. And of course, we could use it for good – it could be a great tool for evolution, curing prejudice and bad taste," Parker says with a smile. He turns to see Gavin come through the doorway. Everyone exchanges glances, and the conversation stops.

"You can really get lost in this place," Gavin says. His black sneakers move like a panther across the floor.

"We were just finishing a discussion," Parker comments casually. "Are you getting restless?"

"Not at all," Gavin's bright eyes are unflinching, and they penetrate through the dark strands of hair falling over them.

Ana wipes her eyes, and sniffs a bit.

"Mom, please don't cry," Patrick pleads. "I'm gonna be totally fine. The Valencia can't lay a finger on me. You have to believe me."

"Can we talk about this later?" Ana asks glancing at Gavin. "I think we could all use some time to think this through."

We walk back to the commons area and while Patrick is consoling his mom, I catch Gavin's eyes staring at me in the shadows under the Tree of Life.

There is seaweed salad and root vegetable soup for lunch. Ana is busy distracting herself with her notes, and I am busy pretending like I don't notice Gavin's staring problem. Every time I catch him looking at me, my stomach does a couple of back-flips – and not the "I'm so excited" kind, but the "stop creeping me out" sort. Why does he make me so nervous?

"Amy, can we meet up in the meditation chamber after lunch?" Ana asks while clutching at her pile of notes and a large mug full of tea. I jump at the chance to put some distance between myself and Mr. McStares-alot.

"Sure," I say.

"You too Patrick. I have some theories I need to test."

"Really? Because I have some theories of my own that I would really like to test with Amy," Patrick says seductively. Reaching his arm around my waste, his lips find their way to my neck. Option number two is sounding pretty good.

"No, seriously. I need your help with this," Ana commands.

"Okay, mom. We'll be there," Patrick caves.

"I don't mind," I tell him.

Parker chimes in, "You have to understand, it's hard not to feel like a lab rat. Patrick has been involved in his mother's experiments his whole life."

"I know it makes her happy," Patrick says with a sigh.

Gavin smirks, "Do you do everything that makes your mommy happy?"

There is an awkward silence, and I can see the faint outline of a vein rise on Patrick's temple. He glares at Gavin like he wants to punch him in the face. These two aren't going to be bffs anytime soon. Parker breaks the silence with a cough.

"Gavin, would you like a tour of Entael? Or we could go on a nature walk. I think there's an eagle's nest down the hill. Yes, actually, I can see it right now. Two little eaglets…

"I'll take a tour of the place," Gavin says nonchalantly. "I've never seen so many curved walls in my life."

"You really should see it from above. It's surreal to say the least," Parker comments leading Gavin to the center dome.

I squeeze Patrick's hand to calm him down and lure him to the meditation chamber. As we step over the curves of lines embedded with sand I can feel his pulse slow down. The wooden ceiling heightens the smell of cedar I sense on Patrick and I resist the temptation to run my lips across his neck.

"Thanks guys. I know there are a lot of other things you could be doing," Ana says warmly. She doesn't know the half of it. "To start, I would actually like Amy to exit the room so I can first test Patrick alone.

"Okay, I'll just be next door," I say giving Patrick's hand a gentle squeeze. I stroll casually into the Tree of Life dome only to see Gavin and Parker standing near the trunk. I try to duck back into the meditation chamber, but it's too late – Parker has seen me.

"Amy, darling, are you attempting to escape from the prying eyes of science? Well, join us then. We were just discussing the nature of nature. This tree here, she has the finest proportions – a real knockout. And just feel that bark – stunning."

"It is a beautiful tree," I say walking over. I avert my eyes to avoid Gavin's gaze.

"The Tree of Life," Parker continues. "There is something magical about her. Many believe it is her energy that makes Entael unseen by normal perception."

"This tree is special isn't it?" Gavin asks slowly walking his hand across the bark of the trunk, and I notice all of the birds chirping wildly as they fly off the tree. "You can almost feel it," he adds glancing over at me. My stomach lurches into a free-fall, and I look anxiously over my shoulder toward the meditation chamber. As if to answer my desire, the door opens and Ana's head pokes out.

"I'm ready for you now," she says cheerfully.

"I'll see you guys later," I say almost skipping my way back to the meditation chamber.

"So, I have just checked and confirmed that Patrick's coding ability is normal. He is able to align the grains of sand on this tray into lines going up and down and then to lines running side to side. I want to re-test it when you are focusing your attention near him," Ana says.

"Okay, I'll try," I take a deep breath and feel the air filling my lungs. I feel a pulse of energy undulate in the air, and my back arches slightly as I look up to see the concentric circles of wood echo their pattern into my thoughts. When I look down, Patrick has aligned the sand into the same pattern of concentric circles. I start to feel time slowing down, and I can sense the entire room shift, everything feels lighter, less dense. Patrick turns his gaze to the lines of sand embedded in the floor and I see they are moving – like rivers. My heart thumps in my chest and I can see Patrick's face concentrated on the sand; he looks motionless. I feel the wave of energy flowing between us intensify as the sand in the room rises, dancing into concentric patterns in the air. His eyes are so focused – he doesn't even register when I kiss him slightly on his cheek. I watch Patrick's mouth expand into a smile, and feel the grains of sand returning to their origins as time speeds up.

"That was amazing," Ana exclaims. "It is just as I thought. Your perceptual shift enables a heightened degree of coding – fascinating. Did you notice your hand becoming translucent?"

"No, I just felt really light, almost weightless," I say.

"Have you been able to influence matter before you met Patrick?" Ana asks.

I think about it for a minute. The time on the tennis court was the first time I'd experienced anything like this, and I was playing against Patrick. "Actually I haven't. It's only been since I met him," I say.

"Well, I don't want to brag, but I'm pretty awesome, so..." Patrick says gleaming.

"Shut-up!" I say playfully pushing him back. I grab his shirt to pull him back. "Okay, maybe you are a little bit awesome.

Ana's thoughts fall over each other racing out of her mouth at one hundred and eighty miles per hour. "This could reinforce the idea that coders trigger coding in others – or that couples can come to enhance each other's influence on the environment. I wonder if gender affects it? Will you let me know if you are able to shift matter without Patrick? You must have affected the density and weight of material to make the sand rise– this explains so much, and leaves even more questions. We need to do more tests..."

"Okay mom, maybe later," Patrick says taking my hand and leading me out.

"Love you!" Ana calls out distractedly as she scratches some mathematical formulas onto her notepad.

"Hey, did you kiss me back there? Cause I feel like you did but I didn't see you do that," Patrick asks. He looks confused like someone stole his wallet.

"Yea, I totally kissed you. You didn't even see me," I say laughing. I don't know why, but I can't help but feel incredibly pleased with myself right now, like I just won a million lotteries. I'm definitely going to have to control the urge to do this all the time.

Chapter 11

"Can you smell that?" Patrick asks sniffing under his arm. "That is ripe. You know it's bad when you can smell yourself. I have to do something about this."

I lean over and wrap my arms around his waist. "I think you smell good – like a tree growing from a rock, surviving hot desert days and cold desert nights."

"Really? Like a tree uh?" he says taking a second sniff. "I'm glad you find my body odor inspiring, but I think this tree could use a little shower."

He squeezes my hand and disappears behind the shower room door. I go for a cup of tea, head to the commons area and find a seat at a table by the window. The hot water steams the scent of green tea leaves and jasmine and I gaze out the window through the veil of steam to see a coyote winding his way across the hill. He walks easily across the rocky terrain, as if he knows every rock under his feet. With my attention distracted by the coyote, I barely perceive the presence of someone sit down across the table. It is Gavin. His amber eyes stare at me across the table. I decide it is time to confront the problem upfront, and I force myself to return his gaze.

"What is your deal?" I ask. "Do you have some kind of staring problem?" He shrugs his shoulders and flashes me a glance that is almost condescending. "Okay, well, I need you to stop. It's unnerving."

His eyes stare more resolutely, without shame. "Are you sure you want me to stop?" he asks quietly.

"Yes. I'm sure." I say holding out in this massive staring contest.

"'Cause I don't think you really want me to," he explains.

Something about his reply sets me off. "Look, if you don't stop, I will walk away from every encounter with you from this moment on," I say in my most piercing tone.

Gavin continues to gaze into my eyes, searching for something. "Alright, you win. I'll stop," he says casually, averting his glance to the wooden fibers of the table. His finger runs along one of the rings across the surface. "It's because of him isn't it. And how long have you known him?"

"Patrick? About a week," I say hesitantly. To say it out-loud sounds odd. I feel like I've known him for months, maybe even years, and it's only been a week.

"That's not that long," he counters. "It can't be that serious."

Feeling like I just tried to buy something I couldn't pay for, I struggle to maintain my ground. "We are having a living creature..." I finally say proudly. The look of confusion on his face fades into one of knowing. "It's not what you think," I say quickly.

"A living creature? Really. What kind of living creature?" he asks tapping the table.

"You'll have to ask Patrick. It's his thing," I reply.

He sits back in his chair, and his expression softens. His eyes gaze openly, and his tone is lighter, more authentic. "How long are you staying?" he asks.

"Just until Friday, we have school on Monday," I say.

"Exactly how old are you?" he asks with genuine curiosity.

"Seventeen." I watch his contort slightly. "That's right. It may not even be legal for you to be staring at me. I should have just got a lawyer," I joke.

His eyes light up in a flash. "Lawyers couldn't have stopped me," Gavin laughs. I sit back, stunned a bit by his comment. "I could have sworn you were at least twenty," he comments.

We both turn to hear the sound of Parker shuffling a stack of cards. "Anybody up for a game of poker?" he asks.

"I'm down," Gavin shrugs.

"Down for what?" Patrick says approaching the table. "Oh I see – Parker wants to play some cards. Of course he does."

"What do you mean? Everyone likes a little game of chance once in a while," Parker winks.

"Fine. Let's play a little game of 'chance'," Patrick replies sitting down next to me. His hair still wet, it sticks out in a hundred different directions. I reach up to tame the beast, and manage to get at least one rogue piece to stay down.

Parker takes out a briefcase full of poker chips. We each get a stack of chips, and then he deals everyone two cards. "Don't pick up your cards directly," Patrick warns me. "Parker can see them. We have to get a look and keep them face down like this." He slides his cards barely off the table and quickly puts them back. I repeat the motion, and barely glimpse a 7 and a 2 below my fingertips. I look over to see Parker looking at his own cards upright in his right hand.

"Who is in?" Parker asks confidently sliding four chips to the center.

Patrick and Gavin both toss chips into the center. "I'm out," I say turning my cards over to Parker.

Three more cards are dealt onto the table, two queens and a jack. Parker moves a short stack of chips to the center, and Gavin quickly follows suit.

"I'm out," Patrick tosses his cards over to Parker. "Don't look at my cards – not that you haven't already."

"Patrick, please! I don't have to cheat to beat you at poker," Parker smiles. He lays another card on the table, and then pushes another short stack onto the pile. Gavin hesitates, and finally matches his stack in the center. The final cards show Parker with two pairs – kings and queens. Gavin was betting on two jacks and an ace. Parker's grin is almost maniacal as he pulls the pile of chips to his corner. The second round of cards is dealt and I look to see an eight and a nine. When Parker starts the bet with four chips I match him.

"Is that really wise? I wouldn't bet with that," Patrick whispers in my ear.

"Now, now, Patrick. If I'm not to look at cards, why should you be reading people's thoughts? That hardly seems fair," Parker scolds.

"I'm just giving some advice – Amy's not used to playing with us yet," Patrick says innocently.

"Fine. Shall we continue?" Parker asks dealing three cards on the table: a six, a seven and a king. All I need is a five for a straight. I raise the bet by four chips. Patrick and Gavin follow. The last two cards turn to reveal an ace and a four.

"I got nothing," I shout throwing down my cards.

"That's quite the poker face," Gavin says with a smile revealing a pair of aces.

"Oh, shut up," I taunt. Even as I try to play it cool, I can feel the emotion rising in my chest. My focus shifts to the cards shuffling between Parker's hands. I can see them in slow motion, collapsing into each other. Ace, four, nine, king... Patrick smiles and directs his attention to the shuffled deck. I can see them sliding in-between each other, slipping into a different pattern. The motion slows almost to a stopping point and I see an ace of hearts. Parker deals the cards.

"You just dealt the cards in reverse order," Gavin complains.

"Did I?" Parker questions. "Well, no matter. Who wants in?" He smiles and closes his eyes. I can tell he is looking at my cards – the ace of hearts, and a jack of spades. I focus on the deck in his hand and notice him burn two cards on accident before dealing the cards to the table. A second ace, a king, and a ten is placed on the table.

"I'm all in," I say, pushing all of my chips to the center.

"So am I," Patrick says. Gavin looks at Parker with a flash of anger. "Why did you deal him my cards?"

"I'm not sure that I did. You worry too much. Just play the game," Parker barks.

Patrick lays his cards down to reveal a jack and a queen. He has a straight flush. He stifles his smile as he pulls in the pile of chips. Gavin's eyes dart between us. "You are all cheaters," he shouts. All at once, every card on the table lights up in flame.

Gavin pushes his chair from behind him and storms away from the table. Patrick presses his hand down on the flames and Parker flings the flaming pile in a vain attempt to pick up the burning the cards. I run to the kitchen and grab a carafe of water, and come back to find a small fire lit on the center of the table. The water is singed by the flames, reducing them to a thick cloud of smoke. We struggle to breathe through the fits of coughing. Patrick opens the door and the windows to greet the fresh evening air, and slowly the smoke dissipates.

"What the hell was that?" Patrick demands.

"We cheated," I reply.

"I didn't mean to – I was just thinking about getting a good hand," Patrick says.

"Is that why I dealt the cards wrong?" Parker realizes. "I could have sworn it was just an accident."

"I felt time slowing down. I could see every card you shuffled. We definitely cheated."

"So you light the place on fire? I didn't know that was possible. How is that possible?" Patrick asks looking at Parker.

"Don't look at me – I didn't know he was a flame-thrower," Parker comments.

"You can't read him either can you." Patrick accuses. "I've been trying since he got here."

Parker shakes his head. "There is a sort of blockade there, but that's common in highly intelligent people. I didn't think anything of it," he replies.

"Well I don't trust him," Patrick states.

"He's a good kid," Parker counters. His eyes look exhausted, and for the first time he seems older, worn out. He makes his way in the direction where Gavin took off. "Let me talk with him. He'll come around," he says warily.

I help Patrick clean up the last of the burnt cards. I realize that Gavin is slightly crazy, and has the ability to light things on fire. I also know that most girls would find him irresistible, and because of this he is kind of a sleaze monster, but I sensed something good in him, something under the surface, where no one else could see. I turn to look at Patrick. "We should give him a chance. Maybe it's our suspicion that makes him hard to read. We are all connected right?"

He lets out a long groan of resistance, and runs his fingers through his wet hair, shaking it off. Patrick somehow knows I'm right. "It's just hard to trust someone you can't read," he says shaking his head. "And I can't stand the way he stares at you," he confesses. Cradling my face in his hands, he searches my eyes for a response.

"I know. You don't have to worry, I took care of that," I say gently kissing his lips.

"Come on." Patrick takes me by the hand and leads me out of the common's area into the cool night air. The sun has completely set, and the moonlight illuminates the rocky outline of a narrow path. I run my fingers along the rough curvature of passing boulders and follow his steps cantering down, letting gravity pull us forward. Slowly, the shadows reveal intricate lines where the leaves meet branches as my eyes adjust to the dark. I can hear the rush of moving water somewhere through the trees. "This is it," he says stopping. The dark pool of water gleams in the moonlight. Patrick's smile is contagious and I can almost picture the little boy sneaking out at night to come down here. "You have to be careful, it can be kind of hot," he warns taking off his shirt. He pulls his shoes off and my heart skips a beat as I tug on the button of my jeans. I breathe a sigh of relief to see that I'm wearing my turquoise underwear – in the dark they almost pass for a swimming suit. I self-consciously keep my led zeppelin t-shirt on and follow Patrick into the steaming hot pool. My feet grasp the river stones under the water and I struggle to keep my balance; the rough texture of the stone tickles the inner soles of my feet. Patrick catches my arm and I find my way to a large piece of limestone. I take a deep breath and sink into the steamy dark water.

"This is really nice," I sigh. I close my eyes and run my fingers along the soft surface of the water. My shirt billows out, and flaps like a sail under the water against my skin. I feel Patrick's hand grasp my fingertips and turn to feel his lips on my neck. His hand vanishes under the water and finds its way to my waist, winding slowly up my rib cage underneath the black angel on my shirt. Feeling blind in the dark, my fingertips reach for his chest, slowing exploring the curving convergence of muscle and bone. Looking into his eyes, I'm overwhelmed by my affection for every part of him, and I feel my eyes well up with tears from the tenderness overtaking my heart.

"What's wrong?" he asks pulling back slightly. "Is this too much?"

"No," I say holding onto his wrist. "My heart is just overactive. It's all good." I pull him closer and rest my lips near his mouth. He can't stop smiling, and I attempt to nudge his lips into a kiss.

"Are you sure?" he asks.

"Yea, I'm sure." Suddenly I feel light-headed, and I stand up to break out of the heat of the pool. "I think it's getting really hot," I say. I squeeze the water out of my hair and then realize my wet shirt is clinging to my chest.

"Yea, it is," he sighs with a smile moving to sit up on a rock near the edge. I scoot up onto a ledge, and tug on my shirt to shake some of the water out. "You know, for all of the meditation and transcendental experiences I've had at Entael, this is the place I feel the most peace. Just sopping wet on this rock, totally helpless and content."

"I feel like one of those Japanese snow monkeys who spend all day soaking in the hot springs," I comment.

I sense the image of a wavy line and I can tell Patrick is communicating without words, that words are meaningless somehow, and the ability to think recedes into the distance. What is left is the pure perception of the world around me and everything feels blurred somehow. The air tastes more delicious and everything seems perfect and alive. A laugh stumbles out in amusement at the thought of Amy Kitcher – what a silly dream that was. To think there is anything other than all of this together seems really funny somehow. The laughing is contagious and slowly we become delirious with it; we laugh uncontrollably and all I feel is relief and joy. After watching in complete awe at the trees swaying in the breeze, we smile at one another like newborns. Patrick takes a deep breath and exhales slowly. He places his hand gently on top of my head, and looks into my eyes.

"Amy? We have to pull it together. There is a danger to talking without words, and I need you to come back."

"I don't want to – what's the big deal?" I can feel my identity coming back slowly as the words form in my mind, with all of its binds and ties and longings.

"Look, this is always here for us, but there is a risk that we won't want to talk anymore, that we'll lose our sense of ourselves and so it's important to go back and forth." Patrick's tone is soft as he coaxes me back.

I raise my legs up out of the water and find my bearings to stand on both feet. I can feel the breeze sweep across my back, leaving goose-bumps across my shoulder blades. "But it's all so beautiful – how can that be dangerous?" I ask shivering.

"Here, take the wet shirt off and put on mine," he says handing me the soft handful of his white cotton t-shirt. I hesitate for second and then take him up on the offer. "It's not dangerous if you come back, but speaking without words amplifies meditation, and sometimes it's hard to come back. People just drift in contentment, blending in with the world, and they forget their old lives. It used to happen all the time with the monks here."

"Maybe that's not so bad... Maybe people should be blending in with the world... Who are you to stop them?" I ask, my teeth clattering in the cold night air.

"You're right. It could be good. It could also put people in a vulnerable state and I just want you to have the ability to do both," he says taking my hand. "Come on, we have to sneak back in. It's way past bedtime at Entael."

I ponder the ethics of transforming human consciousness as we make our way back up the hill. As the leaves shift into focus, somehow the night feels different, like a friend departing and I am sad to see it go. We sneak into Entael still dripping wet from the hot-springs and leave a trail of water back to our beds. Patrick kisses me goodnight and I change into dry shorts and settle under the covers, attempting to put my thoughts to rest.

In between fits of restless sleep I dream I am jumping off of cliffs and flying, somehow propelling myself above the ground. I swerve up and down, controlling my flight and then realize I have wings. Long streaming feathers flap in the air, and I panic as I see them turn black. The next thing I know, they are on fire, burning up high above a mountain range. I fall like a stone, and wake up in a panic before I hit the ground.

Chapter 12

I wake up for the last time from a long night of restless sleep and realize it is Wednesday. It's been three days since I first came here and I'm still waking up a little lost. I lay quietly, thinking about the dreams I had throughout the night. My unconscious must be having a hay-day with all of the stuff that's been going on. I've never felt so powerful and so vulnerable all at the same time. Being able to shift matter and slow time seems so crazy to think about, but when it's happening it seems perfectly normal. Ana's comments from yesterday come back to me – it all started when I met Patrick. Is he the reason I can do these things? Would it have started if I met any coder? I settle under the sheets and close my eyes, still tired, in the dim light under the white fibers. A part of me wants to go back to being just Amy, to being a teenager whose biggest problem was making new friends at school. I hear the sound of voices and lower the sheet to face reality, at least for the morning.

The kitchen is busy. Making some toast and reaching for a spoon I bump into an older woman. It is Grace. Her dark hair looks especially frazzled in the morning sunlight as she stirs some sugar into her tea.

"Good morning dear," she says feigning her best early-morning smile. "How did you sleep?"

"Not great," I say shaking my head. "I don't know what to do with all of my thoughts right now," I confess.

We walk our breakfasts out into the dining area. "That can be tricky," she says. "Try managing other people's sometime! Now there's a conundrum for you."

I exhale a deep sigh and hug my knees up to my chest, balancing a cup of coffee between my fingers. "That does sound intense. How long have you been doing that?"

"Well, since I was just a girl. I kept it a secret for a long time. It was considered an act of witchcraft when I was young," she says laughing. "Still is, in some parts."

I sit up and lean forward, putting my coffee down. "Could you teach me?" I ask hopefully.

Her dark green eyes look at me through the steam billowing out of her tea cup. "Of course," she says. "It is easier to start when you are young."

I sit up to focus on her every word.

"The truth is, you have probably already experienced mind reading, you just didn't know it. People's thoughts drift in and out of our perceptions, and sometimes, it's hard to know whether a thought is ours or not. Of course, people don't realize they are sharing their thoughts – otherwise they might keep better care of what they are thinking!"

I think about this for moment. There have been times when I don't know where some of my thoughts came from, and when I was little I used to share dreams with Ally. I remember thinking it was kind of weird, but somehow I thought that's just what friends do. Grace nods her head as if she knows what I'm thinking, and the funny thing is she actually does.

"That's right, you can share dreams too. All thought is exchanged in a pool of consciousness; some call it the astral plane, others call it a field. You can tap into every memory, perception and wish for the future."

"So, how does this work?" I ask.

"Close your eyes, and observe your thoughts."

I smile and turn my head slightly, questioning her suggestion. She just stares back at me with her big forest green eyes. Reluctantly, I close my eyes. I feel my heart pounding and take a deep breath. My thoughts are streaming images of the past few days. It feels like they are fishing for my attention, as if they are luring me to latch on and continue their path. I breathe deeply and watch them pass. Slowly, small impressions of random emotions surface, and I feel a pull to feel them and have the thoughts they carry with them. I resist the temptation to grasp what feels like hanging threads of emotion. I take another deep breath. I can feel my heartbeat slowing down and sense the space in between my thoughts clearing. Grace's voice enters the space, speaking softly.

"Good. Now take my hand, I want you to sense one of my memories," she says.

I reach out to grasp her warm palm and suddenly sense a wave of light. The sun is shining down brightly, and we are at a park. Children chase each other up the hill and there is a boat drifting out on a nearby lake. The faint spray of mist from the lake hits my face as I walk down to the sandy beach. A man rows the boat inland toward me. His face is tan leather, worn down by years of fishing out in the sun. His gentle smile greets me as he raises his hand to wave. "Grace!" he calls.

I pull back for a second and realize this is a memory from Grace's childhood.

"That was my father," Grace says gently. "My papa – he was always fishing."

Still reeling and a little embarrassed, I look at her apologetically. "I'm sorry," I say.

"No, no, no." She shakes her head and smiles. "Don't be sorry. It is always there – the truth of our lives. There really is no reason for hiding it. No reason for keeping secrets."

"Well, he seemed like a wonderful dad. He loved you very much," I say.

"Aye, he was my favorite. Always taking my side," she says with a deep grin looking up behind me. I turn to see Patrick standing with his finger on his lips shushing Grace.

"Ah Grace – you gave me away! I was trying to sneak up on Amy. She never would have known if you hadn't looked up," Patrick argues.

"Yes I would – I can smell you a mile away," I protest, and playfully squeeze his arm as he sits down.

"Contrary to popular belief, I do bathe regularly," he claims.

"How regularly?" I tease.

"Well – weekly," he qualifies his claim laughing.

"That's quite often," Grace says. "You should have seen the sixties..."

"Dirty hippies," Patrick chides.

"My boyfriend at Berkley could have been mistaken for a medieval peasant if it weren't for his glasses," Grace comments laughing. "I can still smell him now ..."

"Somehow that's one memory I don't think I want to experience," I say with a smile.

"So you are reading memories now?" Patrick asks.

"She's a natural," Grace replies. "Tune her thoughts like a radio dial this one can."

I shake my head in protest. "It was just one time," I say.

"A natural." Grace squeezes my shoulder and smiles a goodbye, making her way back to the kitchen area.

Patrick leans back and places his arm up on the windowsill. "What am I thinking right now?" he challenges.

I lean in so close to his face our noses touch. "I'm not reading your thoughts. I like not knowing with you." I kiss him gently on the mouth. I pull back and he leans forward, yearning for just one more kiss. The next thing I know his arms enfold me and I am pressed back onto the bench struggling to satiate Patrick's hunger for me. Not that I mind. In between kisses, I begin sense his perception and am overcome with the temptation to read his thoughts. I can see myself lying on the bench. Somehow I look beautiful, more beautiful than I've ever imagined looking. It is as if all of me is good, and all of my imperfections never existed. Is this how Patrick sees me? Even the scar under my chin is somehow endearing, and my eyes look more alive, in complete enjoyment. The awareness that we are in public slowly creeps its way back into my perception and I turn to see Ana standing above us.

"Hi mom," Patrick says without looking up. He kisses my mouth lightly one last time before sitting up to face Ana.

Her eyebrow is raised, and she is standing with her arms crossed. I can tell public displays of affection aren't really the norm at Entael.

"Listen, I know you two really like each other. But please be mindful of your location. This is a sacred space for people to find solace and seek enlightenment." Her tone reminds me of the librarians in elementary school.

"I for one am finding solace," Patrick says facetiously.

"I'm really sorry..." I try. I feel sort of like a hussy. I halfway seriously wonder if they make you where the scarlet letters around here. Ana just stares at us, unmoved.

"Okay, mom," Patrick says so obediently Ana releases the tension in her eyebrows and relaxes the tightness in her shoulders. This is just what she needed to hear and he knows it. I can't help but laugh at the fact that I use the same exact tone with my parents.

Her eyes blink to reveal the real anxiety she has been hiding, "I've asked Parker to join us in the meditation chamber. We need to decide what to do about the Indus script. Do you have the missing page with you?"

"Yea," Patrick hesitates. "I'll bring it."

"Thank you. And I would appreciate it if we could not tell anyone else about this."

"Of course," I say quickly. I glimpse Patrick roll his eyes, more than slightly annoyed with his mom as we follow her to the chamber. Patrick heads off toward his living space, presumably to grab the infamous missing page of the Indus script.

Inside the chamber, we find Parker sitting cross-legged on a meditation pillow. I can see his eyes are closed behind the pink lens of his sunglasses, and he appears to be in some kind of trance. Beams of sunlight pour across the room, and I smile slightly at the feel of the sand embedded in the spiraling cracks beneath my feet. We approach Parker quietly and carefully lower our bodies to sit on the hard pillows surrounding him. Patrick comes bouncing into the room carrying a rolled up sheet of old parchment paper. He looks completely calm, while Ana looks exhausted. A slight scowl is wearing itself a permanent home across her brow; lines from worry are creased around her eyes. I am struck by how stressful it must be to be a parent – let alone Patrick's mother. Parker slowly opens his eyes and smiles to greet us.

"I was just viewing the Valencia. I'm happy to report they appear to be in a constant state of strife these days. I saw some particular nastiness between Lucia and his brother, Richard. The only thing they seem to agree on is that they want the remaining piece of the scroll, and they want to see Patrick pay—" Parker hesitates to complete his thought, "with his life." Ana buries her face in her hands, covering tears that stream down her face.

"Mom, please," Patrick says while he rubs her back. "The Valencia get their panties in a wad all the time. I will take care of this. Please, don't cry." Thinking about Patrick being attacked makes my heart race and I rack my brain for a solution. Surprisingly, one actually comes.

"I have an idea," I say quickly. This page of the scroll allows its reader to reproduce thoughts in other people that make them seem as though they are what the person always believed yes?"

"Yes," Parker comments unrolling the script onto the floor. "In theory, the page contains a symbol that innately latches onto a person's current desires, and can be used to make whatever thoughts you want them to believe seem as if they were always there."

"So, why don't we use it to make them believe the scroll was never stolen in the first place? If we could sort of hypnotize the leaders of the Valencia into thinking it never existed, they wouldn't wonder about the missing page." Ana looks up and I see a hint of hope reflected in her eyes.

"That would be a complicated process. We could start by trying it remotely, and then if that fails, we could send Patrick to deliver the message in person," Parker comments. "I'll start working on it this afternoon."

Patrick smiles deviously. "It's brilliant. I love sneaking into the Necoli Castle to steal stuff. But this time, I get to take their thoughts – it's perfect."

"Hold on Patrick," Ana glares. "Parker is going to attempt this remotely first. Haven't you learned your lesson? Messing with the Valencia is not fun. This isn't a game."

"Mom, I know this is hard for you to understand, but life is a game. It is supposed to be fun, and we all have to die someday," Patrick replies. "You have to learn to accept that I don't mind dying. You should have known I wouldn't. You raised me here, in a place frequented by people who taught me the importance of nonattachment. You had to know that at some point I would come to apply this to my life. You have to let me go." Patrick's voice cracks and tears fill his eyes. This is clearly a personal conversation and Parker and I exchange nervous glances as we rise to make an exit.

"Wait," Ana holds my wrist, "you don't have to go. She reaches toward Patrick and waits for him to look up at her. "Honey, I'm sorry. There's no way I'm ever gonna let you go. Someday when you are older you may find yourself caring for someone this way, and then you'll understand," she says smiling with a look of knowing. "You know a good teacher is one who demands everything you've got, and in this way, you are the best guru I'll ever have."

Patrick leans over to embrace his mother. My vision blurs and I can see an image of Patrick as a small boy, coming in with a sharp cut on his knee, and Ana leaning down to hug him, to show him how much she loved him, to show him that he was safe in her arms. Fifteen years later, they hug to help her realize he will always be safe, even if he doesn't live to talk about it. I am moved to tears by their exchange, but I feel out of place, like I stumbled into a counseling session looking for my sweatshirt.

"It's settled then," Parker comments picking up the page from the floor. "I will work on replacing the Valencia's thoughts to believe the scroll was never stolen, and only if I fail will Patrick need to deliver the message in person, or as a last resort, the missing page of the scroll." Ana and Patrick both nod in confirmation.

"Thank you for all of your help," Ana says hugging Parker. "I don't know what we would do without it." She turns to me, and I guess there's hugs all around as she squeezes the air out of my lungs. "Thanks for being here. I think your idea really will work."

"Where is Gavin?" Patrick asks.

"He's sleeping in. He should be up for lunch," Parker comments. "We were supposed to go for a hike. Could you guys entertain him while I focus on this?" Parker asks holding up the page of the scroll.

"Sure," I say trying to be helpful, "why not?"

Patrick starts to comment, clearly wanting to express a host of reasons 'why not'.

Ana interrupts him, "I actually need Patrick's help this afternoon. We have a shipment coming into town that I need to pick up," she explains. Patrick looks less than pleased. "It will only take a couple of hours," she consoles. "I'm sure Amy won't mind entertaining Gavin for just a few hours."

"Sure," I say wondering if anyone notices how unsure I actually feel about this.

Chapter 13

"We'll be back in a few hours," Patrick assures me. He runs his hand along my arm, and stares into my eyes, looking for signs of discontent. "Are you sure you're alright with this?"

"Yea, it's all good," I manage to smile. "Don't worry about me. I'll be fine." He kisses my forehead and is out the door before I open my eyes. I sit down to wait for Gavin to wake up. It feels odd babysitting a grown man, and I can't help but feel a little nervous. Is he even going to want to hang out with me? Or is he still upset from last night? It's not long before I see the jet black hair and dark, brooding eyes approach my table.

"Did you sleep well?" I ask.

He runs his fingers through his hair and sits down across from me. Ignoring my question, he asks, "Have you seen Parker?"

"He has some work to do, and he thought we could hang out while he works."

"Where's your boyfriend?" he replies turning his gaze up to look me in the eyes. I return his stare and feel my pulse increase slightly. I thought we had taken care of this. Why does this guy send me into fight or flight mode every time he looks me in the eye?

"He had to go run some errands for Ana. They'll be back in a few hours," I say crossing my arms. I have to resist the temptation to tell him off.

"What did you have in mind?" he asks.

"We could go for a hike," I offer politely.

"Alright, I could use a break from this place. Too many vacant smiles and if I have to say 'Namaste' one more time I swear," he says.

The sunlight seems brighter than usual and the smell of pine trees is interwoven with the sound of birds chirping. A soft breeze follows us down the ledge to a rocky path winding up through the foothills. We walk in silence stepping carefully over the dust covered rocks lining the path. I notice a hawk circling in the air above us and point her out to Gavin. We both jump as she swoops down and flies so close I can feel the beating of her wings through the air.

"That was amazing," I say wide-eyed, catching my breath. We continue to walk and I notice she seems to be following us in the air. After climbing up a steep hill we stop to gaze out over the mountainside. The hawk perches in a nearby pinon tree, and watches us.

I look over to see Gavin's face smiling in contentment. I see a hint of the kindness I felt in him before, and I sense the ability to read his thoughts. It feels awkward at first, sort of like reading someone's diary. I close my eyes and see a tall blonde woman with the same amber-colored eyes as Gavin. She looks sad and flustered as she argues with a dark-haired man, his mother and father. They don't see that Gavin is hiding behind a door. The woman shouts angrily, "it's too far. You went too far. I can't support this anymore. I just can't do it anymore." She reaches for a set of keys on a nearby table and storms out of the room. After the door slams behind her, I can feel Gavin's pain; he somehow realizes he will never see her again. I can feel the heartache rising in his tiny chest. He couldn't be more than five years old.

The memory fades, and I open my eyes to hear Gavin clearing his throat. I can tell by the peaceful look in his eyes, he doesn't know I read this memory. I contemplate telling him, but he speaks before I get the chance.

"Listen, I'm sorry about last night – I don't know what happened," he says quietly.

"No, I'm sorry. We shouldn't have cheated. That was just dumb," I say quickly. I look over, and try to hide the pity I sense for him. I can't imagine losing my mother like that. "So you don't normally run around lighting things on fire?" I ask playfully.

"No, I can't explain what happened," he says shaking his head. "I've never been able to do that before."

I take a deep breath. "I think I know what happened," I confess.

He gazes over at me, his eyes full of curiosity. "What?"

"I have the ability to slow down time, and Ana says this makes it easier to code matter. I don't know exactly how it works, but when I focus on something it gets lighter – more fluid. I think I was doing it last night in the card game, and I think maybe that made it possible for you to light the cards on fire," I say carefully. I look over expecting to see Gavin full of shock or disbelief. Strangely, he doesn't seem surprised. His eyes accept my secret with an awareness I didn't anticipate.

"So you make it easier to 'code matter'," he says. "Can you change events that have already taken place?" he asks intently.

I hesitate to reply. "No, I don't think so," I say. "It's just a shift."

"Show me," he says. His tone is calm, but precise and demanding.

"Fine," I reply. I look over to see the hawk still perched on the nearby tree. She turns her head slightly and I notice the speckles on her feathered neck are layered in a perfect camouflage with the tree branch. She blinks her eyes in slow motion and I sense the lightness fill the air and envelope the earth beneath our feet. Everything seems more alive, and I look over to see Gavin close his own eyes. I jump back as a trail of dry grass lights on fire in a circle around him. He opens his eyes to reveal small flames of dancing embers reflected in his eyes. I remember the drawing I did in class last week; it was Gavin. I somehow knew of him then. How is that possible? He smiles as the flames die off into smoking spirals. I give him a weak smile. I don't know why but I feel embarrassed.

"Very cool," he acknowledges, with a nod of his head. "So you can do that anytime?" he asks.

"Somehow this doesn't seem like news to you. Are you a 'coder'?" I ask trying to avoid his question.

He laughs out loud. "Only quantum physicists hiding out in their labs call it that. They know whoever observes reality first changes its course of action. They are right about that. They just don't know the full extent of this influence."

"What is the full extent?" I ask.

"The expectation that the world is concrete and that reality is stable is so ingrained in the fibers of most human beings, they can't imagine the power to create reality. The truth is, they are too small minded to comprehend it and prefer to live in a world that is given than to take the right to create a new one."

You can almost feel the arrogance dripping off Gavin's tongue as he speaks, and I feel my stomach turn. "Small minded? Really? And what makes you so different?" I ask peering sharply into his eyes.

His laugh is tempered by a coldness in his eyes which stare unflinching back at me. "I've always been different, never really had a choice in the matter." His tone softens and he smiles slightly. A butterfly teeters through the air and lands on his hand. I notice the hawk staring intently at the insect as it stretches its wings. Gavin carefully lifts the fragile creature up. "Do you see this?" he asks.

"She's beautiful," I say.

"Watch carefully," he replies. I stare in shock as the insect lowers her wings and falters before collapsing and lying dead on his palm. A loud call from the hawk permeates the air before I see her take off.

"You – you killed her," I stutter. I take a step back and look at him in disbelief.

"Calm down," he chides. "I said to watch carefully." I look in amazement as the tiny wings move slightly and witness the creature come back to life. "I have the power to both take life and give it back," he comments casually.

"How is that possible?" I ask trembling. My instincts tell me to run away, and I have to force myself to stand there next to him.

"An old family secret," he replies. He looks over to see the stunned look on my face. "Amy, please, don't be afraid," he pleads taking my hand. "I never would have told you—this is a secret, you can't tell anyone. I thought you would understand. Please, please don't go." Gavin's eyes are welling up with tears, and I remember the image of his mother abandoning him. Did she leave because of this? I take a deep breath and decide what to do next.

"It's okay," I say. "I won't tell anyone. But you have to not do that ever again," I demand.

"That's not fair. Would you promise to never slow down time? You don't understand. Sometimes I can't help it."

"Alright, fine. But if you can avoid it, you will right?"

Gavin nods his head. "Yea," he says finally. "I will, for you." I'm both grateful and a little disturbed by this comment.

"Don't do it for me. Do it because it's the right thing to do," I say. He looks out over the horizon. The air pulsates with heat as sun sits low over the mountainside, and I can see him turning my words over in his mind. The storm in his eyes is like a magnetic strobe of lightening.

"What do you know about the "right" thing? What you were taught in school? Did they tell you all the right answers? Do you really think it's that simple? Life is beautiful, but death is too." I open my mouth to reply, but he cuts me off, grasping my shoulders tightly. "Amy, reality can be whatever you want it to be. You see things how they really are – open and malleable. I see things how I want them to be. Together, we could rise up and create a new world, a better world full of people who claim their destiny as creators. It wouldn't matter who tried to stop us."

He looks expectantly into my eyes. I stare back in silence and think of the best way to break the news to him. I don't want to rule the world with him, not with anyone. I just want to have fun and live and play. Before I can speak his hands reach behind by back and pull me toward him. I panic and resist in vain as he presses his mouth against mine. My heart beats in slow motion and I manage to leverage my arms against him, pushing him off of me. I struggle to catch my breath and see through the strands of my hair that hang in disorder like debris from an accident. Gavin looks hurt and confused. Before he can apologize, I raise my hand to silence him.

"Just get away from me," I say fiercely.

"Amy, please," he tries to reason.

"No!" I scream.

He walks away with the hurt look still in his eyes. I am so mad I don't even care. How did that happen? Was it my fault? I shouldn't have read his thoughts. I knew that was wrong. I thought I was so clear that we were just friends, that I wanted to be with Patrick. My thoughts chase each other back and forth as I make my way down the hill back to Entael. I can hear the hawk circling above call out as if to console me. I remember the butterfly lying dead in his hand. Tears flow down my cheeks as I race through the thicket and up past the creek. At the top of the hill I run into Patrick unloading a box from his mom's truck. When he sees that it is me, he instantly stops moving and nearly drops the box full of vegetables.

"What happened?" he asks. Before I can answer, he slides the box back onto the truck bed and rushes to hug me. "Are you okay?"

"I'm fine," I manage to say stifling my tears. I don't want him to worry about this. Why didn't I calm myself down before running back here?

"Was it Gavin? What did he do?" Patrick asks. The anger in his voice punctures the air.

"It's okay – it was just a mistake," I say.

"What was just a mistake? Did he kiss you?" he demands. I shake my head, but the look in my eyes is enough. Patrick nods his head and replies, "I see." His tone is dry and cold, full of tempered rage. I've never seen him like this, veins protruding from his temple, his hands shaking, so out of control. No sign of the peaceful, fun-loving Patrick I love. The large wooden door bursts open and both Ana and Parker file out.

"Parker has some unsettling news," Ana informs us. The concern in her eyes tells us something is seriously wrong.

Parker stammers, "I was working to replace the thoughts of Luca Fieri and I saw memories of Gavin. It turns out Gavin is his son. Luca is Gavin's father."

"I knew he couldn't be trusted," Patrick laments. "And you brought him here."

"I'm sorry." Parker shakes his head in disbelief. "I swear I didn't know."

A rustle is heard in the bushes by the creek. We gaze down the hill to see Gavin's dark silhouette ambling slowly up the path. Patrick sprints down the hill like a runaway train before anyone can say another word.

Chapter 14

I look over to see Ana's face is frozen in panic. Parker takes off down the ledge after Patrick and I follow him. My legs can't move fast enough as I stumble down the hill. I can barely make out the outline of two figures through the layers of tree branches, and see Patrick run straight into Gavin, tackling him and taking them both to the ground. I run faster and feel my legs grow even more unsteady, nearly tripping over each other with each step over the rocky decline. At the bottom of the hill I run into Parker and see Gavin swinging a large tree branch at Patrick's head. Fortunately Patrick ducks just in time and cuts forward into Gavin's side, dropping him onto his back. Patrick's fist plunges downward toward Gavin's face, and Gavin turns his head just in time.

"No! Stop!" I scream. Parker tries to hold Patrick arm.

"Leave him! Let's go!" Parker calls.

Patrick flings him off and falls back as Gavin tackles him onto the ground. They are like wild dogs tearing into each other. My heart beats so fast it skips like a scratched cd. I can't seem to catch my breath from the run down the hillside as panic takes over. I feel the press of a hand on my back and turn to see Ana, her face contorted, standing behind me.

"We have to do something!" Ana calls out to us. We all stand stunted in shock as Patrick ducks another swing from Gavin's fist.

"I knew something was wrong with you!" Patrick yells violently hitting Gavin in the face. Gavin pauses to wipe the blood from his lip, laughing uncontrollably.

"You had no idea," Gavin calls ducking another punch. "None of you knew, so trusting, so blind. Dad knew no one here would suspect me. Too much peace, love and chanting through clouds of patchouli to notice," he calls out still laughing. Patrick tackles him again, sending them both rolling down the hill toward the creek. "You people make me sick – always holding hands and singing kumbaya. Amy deserves better," Gavin sneers, landing a biting punch on Patrick's jaw. Patrick shoves him off, rolling Gavin's back onto the ground.

"You keep your twisted Valencia hands off of her," he demands wrapping his own hands around Gavin's neck. Gavin finds enough air and manages to throw Patrick off of him.

"I should kill you all," Gavin coughs trying to catch his breath. He turns to look at Ana. "My father would thank me for it." Patrick's temper is triggered and the rage in his eyes sends shivers down my spine. The next thing I know Patrick has tackled Gavin into the water of the creek and is holding his head under the cold gentle stream of water. Bubbles of air surface the water as they leave Gavin's lungs. He's dying. Patrick is killing him. I can feel time slowing down as I rush forward.

"No!" I scream. I can see the tiny particles of sunlight dancing in the leaves, as I clutch Patrick's t-shirt, grab his chest and pull him off of Gavin. I can see the look in Patrick's eyes shift from vehemence to confusion.

Gavin rises up out of the water with a look of pure determination and I shudder as I see his hands grasp Patrick's head.

"No! Please no!" I scream.

My words drop like weights as I see Patrick's eyes close and feel his body go limp in my arms. I barely glimpse Gavin's fleeting image as I bury my face in Patrick's chest. Ana's screams pierce the air, and I look up in despair as she pulls his head into her chest crying uncontrollably.

"Not my baby!" she sobs over and over.

I stop for a second and let my thoughts come back into focus. This is my fault. If only Patrick had known. My thoughts are cold and clear in this moment and I rush back up the hill after Gavin. I push through a thicket of trees to take a short cut up the hill, the sharp dry branches tear at the skin on my face and arms. At the top of the hill I gasp for breath.

"Gavin!" I call out. I panic. He's nowhere in sight. I turn in circles, casting my eyes frantically in every direction. Finally, I see him walking up toward the road.

"Gavin! Stop!" I cry. As he turns back I can see his left hand clutches the missing page of the Indus script. "Please!" I call out running toward him. He turns to see me and his eyes deceive him to reveal a slight hint of remorse.

"It's time to go," he says coldly.

"Please, bring him back," I plead. Warm tears pour out of my eyes trying to put out the fire of despair I feel pulsate in my heart. My legs bend under my weight and I fall to my knees onto the ground, grasping at his arm. "Bring him back," I sob. "I'll do anything." For several agonizing moments Gavin doesn't say anything; he just watches me sobbing at his feet. Finally, I hear him clear his throat.

"Okay. I'll do it," he says calmly. I pause for a second as the meaning of his words sink in. "We have to hurry," he adds. I take Gavin's hand and lead him back down the hill. We find Ana crouched over Patrick's body rocking him back and forth. Parker's face is covered in tears as he stares at Gavin in disbelief.

"How could you? This is an abomination of the first of the order!" Parker shouts.

Gavin motions to speak and I cut him off. "Do it now," I say forcefully enunciating each word.

Gavin kneels down toward Patrick, and Ana violently pushes him away. "Get away from him!" she cries.

"Ana," I say gently squeezing her shoulder. "It's okay. He can help." She reluctantly allows Gavin to approach.

Gavin continues to lean over Patrick, placing his hands on Patrick's temples. Within moments Patrick's face stirs with life and his eyes open slowly taking in the world around him. I exhale my relief and lean forward to kiss him. Time slows and I feel his heart beating under my palm. I can sense every part of him return and the golden stream of light connecting us, pulling on our hearts like magnets. His lips become warm and his eyes look even more alive, anticipating every moment.

"Thank god!" Ana exclaims hugging Patrick.

"What happened?" Patrick asks with genuine curiosity. Ana and I look at each other, unable to speak.

"I killed you," Gavin explains. "And then I brought you back."

"What?" Patrick gasps sitting up. "How?" he stutters, "Why?"

"Because I can. Well, look at the time! I really have to be going. It's been lovely seeing you all. Thank you for the warm hospitality," Gavin says coldly. He pauses for second and looks down at me. "You're welcome," he says quietly. I can't speak. My thoughts sputter like a dying engine as he walks away and disappears up the hill. I help Patrick to his feet.

"Are you okay?" I ask. Patrick clutches at his side and winces in pain, but he manages to smile.

"Never better," he says.

"We should get you up to a bed," Ana exclaims helping him limp toward the path. I stop moving as I remember the image of the scroll in Gavin's hand.

"He has the Indus script," I say.

"What?" Patrick demands.

"This is all my fault," Parker laments. "I can't believe I trusted him."

"We have to stop him," Patrick says weakly, limping slightly faster up the hill. I cringe at the sight of his pain spreading across his face. I can feel time slow and my heart beats quicken.

"I'll handle this," I say sprinting up the hill.

At the top of the hill, something tells me to look inside Entael, and I run through the commons room into the streaming sunlight flowing over the Tree of Life. The room is silent and I'm relieved to see Gavin standing below the tree. I rush to his side and watch in slow motion as he reaches out to touch the thick bark of the trunk. The canopy of bright green leaves fade into waves of brown and gold. Birds cry out as they fly out of the windows lining the ceiling. The light in the room dims and I can feel the air flatten. Even the walls look grey, like regular concrete.

"What have you done?" I ask.

Clearly pleased with his deceit, he grins maniacally, his eyes ablaze. I can feel tears welling up as I stare in disbelief at the branches shriveling above us.

"Just a little goodbye present," he answers. "Think of it as crowd control. No more secret hideout for meddlers getting in our way. We've been wanting to take this place down for decades, but we never knew exactly where to find it, until now."

"Don't leave like this," I ask. He tilts his head slightly, contemplating my request.

"You should come with me. There is no future with these people."

"This tree is sacred. You know it is," I plead.

"Everything has to die sometime. I'm just speeding up the process," he says laughing. "Too bad you can't slow time enough to stop me," he says nonchalantly.

Suddenly it occurs to me, maybe I can. I stare back at him and feel the room shift into focus. It is as if I put on glasses to correct my vision, and I can feel the vibration of each tiny particle. My entire being seems suspended off the ground and I can see myself in the reflection of Gavin's eyes which stare blankly at me, frozen in time. The air is full of tiny dancing crystals of light and as the room becomes luminous I can feel myself becoming translucent – am I disappearing? I am at one with every other particle in the room, and definitely can't see my body, but somehow I am not scared. I gently redirect the course of events, slowly blurring time into a new space. I feel a wave of light blow throughout the room as the Tree of Life bursts with living energy. Its majestic radiance permeates the room. Gavin disappears for a moment and reappears exiting out the heavy wooden door as I feel time quicken. I feel faint and rest my back against the trunk of the tree. I did it. I reversed time. There is a sound of another door opening, and I hear Patrick's voice echo across the room.

"Amy? Are you in here?" he asks.

"I'm over here," I call out.

"Amy?" Patrick wonders across the room and finds me slumped up against the tree trunk, looking a little dazed. "Amy, what's wrong?" he asks. His face stares at me, alarmed. "You look see-through."

"What?"

"I can see through you," he says panicking. I feel his hand come in contact with my wrist and for a second it slips through. I breathe into my lungs and my heart beats return, pounding my chest, connecting the outline of my body.

"I'm right here," I say. My skin is covered in goose-bumps, and tears pour down my cheeks. "I think I need some vitamins." Patrick laughs and hugs me tightly. The weight of his body against me feels good, as if it is stabilizing me.

"Don't ever run off like that again," he says holding me tighter. My thoughts return slowly at first, inching their way back into my mind.

"Gavin left. He killed the tree, and then I reversed time, and saved it. But now he's gone, and he took the script."

"He left just now?" Patrick asks. "We can catch him."

"No, let him go," Ana says. Ana and Parker step carefully over the roots of the Tree of Life. They both have their arms crossed and look like entombed Egyptian pharaohs, stoic, wide-eyed, and completely serious. "It doesn't matter now. All that matters is you're both safe," Ana comments. Parker nods his head in agreement.

"A little newsflash my boy, Gavin has the power to kill you. He did it once today already remember? I'm not about to let him near any of you," Parker says. "It was my fault he came here and I'll be handling him from now on."

"You said he killed the Tree of Life?" Ana asks. She kneels down to feel the roots between her feet. "And you saved it?"

"Yea, I guess I did," I say smiling faintly.

"So you reversed time to a state where the Tree would live," Ana says.

"I think so."

"Mom, I want you to check Amy's vitals. Something really weird happened. You're not going to believe this, but she was like a ghost – totally see through. That's not really normal is it?"

"Is this true?" Ana asks. I nod my head. "This happened before. You said your hand became translucent. Your consciousness unbinds energy from its typical state, but somehow you were able to reposition molecular structure, reconvening it to a prior state. And your entire body was invisible?"

"It was as if I disappeared into the air."

"That's troubling," Ana confirms. "I don't want you to test this any further until we understand what's happening with you. Do you understand?" I quickly nod my head like I'm at the doctor's office taking orders. I don't want to alarm anyone, but it was definitely more than a little troubling to feel like I might not get my body back.

"Let's get you to the living quarters. You need to rest. I want you both in bed, and I mean it." Patrick looks at me and smiles in anticipation. "Your own beds, Patrick, your own beds," Ana clarifies.

As we walk back to the living quarters I gently cradle Patrick's hand, letting relief find its way into my heart. I turn back to glimpse the Tree of Life, and am comforted to see a cluster of bluebirds perched on the upper branches, the Tree's radiant glow flowing throughout the room, as if it never stopped.

Chapter 15

Ana hooks me up to a heart monitor and patrols the living quarters like a watchdog. Every hour she checks to make sure we are resting in bed. Periodically, flashes of blinding light envelope my vision, vaguely reminiscent of the migraines I used to get in junior high. I notice they are followed by loud beeping spikes on the monitor, and wonder if that is normal. I drift in and out of sleep as the light fades into shadow. My thoughts cycle between images of Patrick lying dead on the floor, and Gavin's fingers reaching for the Tree of Life. I keep reminding myself that everything is alright. Patrick is alive. But it feels like a dream. Everything could so easily have gone differently. What kind of power is it to take life? Why didn't I just tell Patrick when I had the chance?

After a particularly disturbing dream haunted by the flames in Gavin's eyes, I wake to see streams of daylight make their way across the room, signaling a new day. It's Thursday, and for the first time after waking up here I know exactly where I am. I also know exactly where I want to be – home. I want to go home.

As I change into my jeans and a t-shirt I notice the sound of commotion from the living quarters and am surprised by the crowd of people bustling around the space. There are numerous orange-robed monks intermingled with tie-dyed t-shirts and everyone seems to have misplaced their shoes. The atmosphere in the room is incandescent and I can almost feel the waves of energy pulsing the air as I pass by each smiling face. I notice Patrick sitting with Ana and Remi at a table across the room and make my way through the cloud of palpable love to meet them.

"Good morning sunshine," Patrick says. His lip is still swollen and he has a dark circle under his right eye. He reaches his arm around my waist and for a second we lose track of the rest world and just hold each other. Ana forces a cough which brings us back to focus.

"How are you feeling?" she asks.

"Better, like a whole person again."

"You gave us quite a scare. Whatever you did, it did a number on your heart rate. Promise me you won't try that again. At least not until we understand how to make it safe," Ana demands.

One thing you could say about being at Entael, there's a lot of promising not to do stuff here.

"I wasn't planning on it," I say reassuringly.

"The power to turn back time is not something to wink at," Remi comments. "We are all very grateful, but it comes not without a cost. That kind of power has vast prarabdhaic karmic impacts." I nod my head like I know what he's talking about, and hope that whatever prarabbiatic means, it isn't too serious. "We have much work to do, if we are to coordinate the attentions of all the people," Remi says joyfully.

"I think Grace will be in this room. She has a special affinity for it," Ana says.

"I plan to join the festivities in the hall of light," Remi says continuing a boisterous smile.

"What's going on?" I ask.

Remi smiles even wider – I didn't think it was possible, and spreads his arms out as if to embrace the air. "It is a beautiful day, and there is much to celebrate," he says. I give Patrick a funny look, and he stifles a laugh.

"No, really, why are all of the people here?" I ask. Ana looks seriously across the table, and my smile fades. I sit carefully down at the table.

"Now that the Valencia know about Entael, it is vulnerable. The power that Gavin holds is beyond anything we could have anticipated," she says. I move uncomfortably in the chair, feeling guilty about the way we could have anticipated.

"Where is Gavin? Do we know?" I ask.

"Parker has been remotely viewing him throughout the night, and he is headed back to the Necoli castle, presumably to bring the missing page of the Indus script back to his father," Ana replies.

"This means he has the power to influence our thoughts yes?" I ask remembering the long night of nightmares plagued by images of Gavin.

"Unfortunately, yes," Ana says. The usual look of concern returns to her eyes. "We all must be on guard with our thoughts from now on. Our thoughts will all seem like our own, but they may be implanted by anyone holding the script. We have to trust that the Valencia have more important things to do then influence then us, and maybe sometime down the road they will come to see the light."

"Mom's an eternal optimist," Patrick comments.

For the first time this morning, Remi looks sober. He stares back at Patrick with a clear intensity that is both calm and vigilant. His words are slow and deliberate.

"Patrick, have some faith," he says. "The path of spiritual transformation comes to us all sometime. Everyone is destined for a little samadhi sooner or later, even the Valencia will come to know it." Patrick shakes his head in amusement.

"I wouldn't hold my breath, Remi," he says.

"You might be surprised my boy. All of these people here walk in some form of divine consciousness. With so many conscious wills directed in this way miracles can happen," Remi replies.

"Is that why they are here? To make miracles?" I ask. Ana smiles patiently at me; clearly I'm the last one to get up this morning.

"We cannot let Entael remain defenseless," she says. Our plan is to hold a ceremony that will raise the vibration of Entael and form a seal of protection. We have invited friends from around the country to come for this purpose."

"It might be just a little bit epic," Patrick says pinching the air between his fingers. His smile veers to concern when he sees the look on my face. "Do you feel up to this?"

"Sure," I say hesitating slightly.

"Because if you don't feel —"

"It's not that. It's just that I miss my mom. I need to go home."

Patrick tries to hide his disappointment with a smile.

"I understand," he says.

"Is there a car I can borrow?" I ask.

"What's this? You are leaving before the ceremony? No!" Remi scoffs.

"Listen, I can't let you go by yourself. The ritual won't take long... what if we stayed just for a bit and then I could drive us home this afternoon? We could be home by tonight," Patrick offers.

I have to admit I am a little curious about seeing some miracles first hand. "Okay, but this time I get to drive," I say.

"Was it really that bad?" he asks.

I stare at him unblinking. He pretends to look hurt. "At least I can obey the laws of the road," I offer.

"Just not the laws of physics," he replies. I can't help but smile remembering the sand in the meditation chamber dancing all around us.

"Amy, are you sure you can't stay?" Ana asks. She reaches over and grasps my hand. "It has been so nice meeting you. You are welcome to visit anytime."

"Thank you. I just really want to see my mom. It's been kind of a long week," I say.

"Of course," she says nodding her head in sympathy.

Suddenly, a stream of hummingbirds enters the room through the open door. They hover over our heads and wisp past our faces. The air seems to purr with their wings and I glimpse flecks of green and purple as they pause in the air watching us. Everyone in the room smiles in amazement.

"They are a good omen," Remi shouts across the table.

"Just amazing," Ana cries.

Patrick squeezes my hand and for a second I forget all about Gavin, Patrick dying and the Valencia as I stare at the buzzing flurry of the tiny winged creatures. Then, as quickly as they came, they fly back outside, leaving us gaping in awe.

People slowly return to their breakfasts and I find myself staring at Patrick. He flinches slightly at the pain of chewing the crunchy flakes of granola, but his eyes still gleam in their usual playful state, surveying the world around him as if every part of it was new. I find myself wondering, yet again, if he is the reason for my abilities, that I wouldn't have been able to slow time if I hadn't met him. Even sitting next to him I can feel the vibration just below the surface, like a soft hum purring in my heart. What would it be like without him? Would I know this part of me if we had never met? There is a curious part of me that would like to run a test to see. I could technically go back in time and play it out with us never interacting couldn't I? I shake my head at the silliness of this idea as Ana and Remi stand up to leave.

"So we'll see you guys at the ceremony yes?" Ana asks.

"Yes. We'll be there. I'm excited for it," I say.

"You can already feel the energy rising can't you? Remi asks. "It is very exciting indeed." He squeezes my shoulder gently and smiles with his eyes. I watch them disappear in the bustle of people coming in and out of the commons area.

Patrick pushes his bowl of granola to the side, stretches his arm across the table and rests his head on his bicep staring peacefully up at me. What do you feel like doing? We have a couple of hours," he asks.

"You look like a cat," I comment, "like you are ready to lounge around."

"If lounging means spending time with you, then yea, I'm ready for it." I reach over and run my fingers through the tangle of blonde hair resting on his arm. He closes his eyes and makes a purring sound in his throat. I laugh and mess up his already disheveled hair.

"I think I should get packed so we are ready to go. And I want to call my mom and let her know I'll be home by tonight. I'm sorry to leave early. I'm just so homesick." Patrick sits up and studies me softly.

"Don't apologize. I miss my mom all the time," he says. I breathe a sigh of relief and lean over to kiss him on the mouth. The lining of tension in my chest dissolves and is replaced by a current of light circling between us. Once again I find myself forgetting the rest of the world and place my hand against his chest to feel his heart pounding.

"What would my life be like without you?" I ask in between kisses.

"Good news is that we don't have to find out any time soon," he says. I feel a small tear roll down my cheek. I smile slightly, a little embarrassed by it.

"It must have been terrifying yesterday. I'm sorry," he says sweeping the tear away. I nod my head and rest it against his chest. "I've never been so angry. I think I let it get to me."

"You think?" I tease.

"I won't let that happen again," he replies.

"How do we return back to the normal world? How do we go back to school?" I ask.

"It's easier than you think. Everything will seem easier to you now, especially because we get to be there together," he says stroking my hair. "It'll be nice to have someone to play with for a change."

"Someone to play with? It sounds like you plan to cause some more trouble. What kind of games do you want to play?" I glare at him teasingly.

"Oh you know, just see how much we can get away with."

"And how do you get away with it? Isn't all of this supposed to be kept secret?" I ask.

"It's true. There's only so much you can do around other people," he says kissing my neck. His fingers running gently down my thigh.

I sense an image of two concentric circles and the words, "not like when we are alone" enter my thoughts. I smile and give him a fake look of disapproval. He grins before kissing my lips fully. I feel a shiver of pleasure run down my spine. He pulls back and ponders my face.

"You said you wanted to pack?" he asks. It takes me a few seconds to return back to the bench at the table in the hall of Entael. The sound of talking, and the scattered images of people moving catch my attention.

"Yes. Packing. Good. I'll get right on that," I say in a daze. A little disappointed by his oddly timed practicality, I feel the pulse in my lower belly beat like a drum. "I think I'll go for a walk and call my mom."

"Sounds good. I'll meet you back here before noon. Do you have a room you'd like to rituate in?" he asks playfully.

"Let's meet in the center, by the Tree of Life." I say.

"Good call," he says kissing my forehead on his way up from the table. "I'll see you in a bit."

I walk back through the waves of patchouli and elated faces to find my bag. Not much to pack – just my tooth brush, my phone, a pair of shorts, a hair brush and my favorite sweatshirt. The clothes are soft and have a thin layer of dirt from being worn all week. It's definitely time to do some laundry. I can't wait to see my mom, and to sleep in my own bed. I have to stifle the part of me that would ditch the ceremony and head back right now. It's just a few hours I tell myself. I can wait.

The air outside is peaceful and the sun sends beads of sweat down my back as I hike up the hill to call my mom. At the top of the hill I catch my breath and survey the landscape. Layers of wild sage blossom across the meadow below. I text Ally to let her know I'll be back at my mom's by tonight. I grasp the phone tight against my ear as I count the rings, waiting for my mom to pick up.

"Hey sweetie, how's it going?" My mom's voice makes my heart ache and I have to swallow the pain of missing her, of lying to her, of having been through so much that she'll never get to hear about.

"It's going good, mom. I've had a great time, but I'm ready to be home."

"Did you and Ally fight? Is everything okay?" she asks.

"Everything's fine. I just want to be home. I'll start just after lunch so I should be home by around nine tonight," I say fighting back the compulsion to cry.

"Okay. That sounds great honey. I can't wait to see you. Drive safe, and call me if you run into any trouble on the road."

"I will mom. I love you."

"Love you too honey."

I hear her voice echo in my thoughts as the phone disconnects. I see a drove of horses push down the hill in a cloud of dust toward Entael. It's the Nektosha. They must be coming for the ceremony.

I reach to put my phone in my back pocket and feel something pull my arm from behind. Before I know what's happening, a gloved hand wraps around my neck and clasps my jaw shut. I struggle in vain to release my right arm from the piercing pain of being pinned behind my back, and watch a long needle dig itself into my left arm. I try to gasp enough air to scream and to keep the blackness from crushing down on me. I can feel my muscles give up, going limp. The gloved hand holding my mouth shut slides its way up to cover my face, and the thick, black blur of fingers are the last things I see before I lose consciousness.

Chapter 16

I wake to see dark burgundy curtains hiding most of the sun's light, and feel my arms tied to curving mahogany arms of a large chair. My heart beat races to the point of hysteria as I remember the needle piercing my vein and realize I've been kidnapped – taken. Tears well up in my eyes and I grind my wrist bones against the metal handcuffs pinning me to the chair. There is something around my neck and I swallow to feel the edge of a cold metal ring. How did this happen? Why do they want me? What could they want me for? What will my mother do? The questions fly through my mind, and I struggle to breathe the cloistered dust-ridden air.

I force myself to calm down and take a deep breath inhaling the lingering scent of cigar smoke. I take a look around the room. The light is faint but I can make out the frame of a large wooden desk. The walls are lined with dusty old books and pictures of men wearing uniforms. A large wooden door stands closed on the other side of the room next to the army of bookshelves. There are several photographs of what look like a class picture of men in college. The wooden floor is covered by a thick black cloak of carpet lined with golden embroidery.

Though my heart beats like a train pounding in my chest, I feel a little better having taken a few deep breathes and gently unwind the tangle of panic in my abdomen to feel a space opening back up inside. Although I don't know what they want with me, I do know I have the power to reverse time. Maybe I can do it long enough to get out of this chair? I remember the danger, what Ana said about my heart rate and how Patrick's hand went through my arm – could I seriously lose track of my body permanently? If only Patrick were here, I could easily loosen the structure of the room long enough for him to break apart the metal clasping my wrists. I laugh a little at my own stupidity. I wanted to test what I could do on my own, and now... now I have to. I pull one more time on my left wrist and feel the pulse of a deep bruise forming around my tendon; the skin is scraped raw revealing tiny red flecks of blood rising to the surface.

I exhale and stare down at my lap. My perception is still hazy from being unconscious but I can focus enough to see the pattern of fabric woven into a tear in my jeans. Lines of white and navy overlap each other in patterns jetting over my knee. I relax further and sense time beginning to slow. Simultaneously, the ring around my neck becomes warm and pulses tiny electric shocks up and down my spine. I sense the colors of room and hear the black carpet in a low drone; the burgundy drapes are like a piercing scream and when I look at the books on the shelf a cacophony of sound erupts in my ears. The feeling of being tied to the chair is a dark cloud that covers my vision and it is all I can do to keep my eyes open. When I give in and close them I let out a cry of frustration and sense the sound of my own sadness in waves of darkened green and gray. I keep my eyes closed and ride out the weird colors that are illuminated every time I take a breath.

Slowly the colors fade and I open my eyes against my arm. The color of my skin is familiar and I can feel myself returning to normal. What happened to me? It has got to be this thing around my neck. It's like the signal just got mixed up, and everything became overly sensed. Tears stream down my face and I taste the salty wet traces on the corners of my mouth.

Suddenly, I hear footsteps and the door in the corner swings open. A tall figure strides across the room carrying something under his arm and I blink the tears out of my eyes to see clearly. He wears a tight, dark grey suit with a blood-red tie bursting at his neck. His eyes seem placed slightly too far apart and stare through me with a piercing ice-colored blue. I force myself to return his gaze and feel the same compulsion to look away as I did with Gavin. I grasp a flash of a memory and realize this man is Gavin's father. I notice the object under his arm is a mesh covered helmet. His face is covered by a long black beard peppered with thick, white coils of hair.

"So, you are awake," he says with a hint of a smile crossing his lips. I swallow to feel the metal ring bound around my neck and carefully try to hide the fear I feel surface in my eyes. "You had a visitor this afternoon. Unfortunately, we didn't see eye to eye so to speak and he had to be ... eliminated."

"What? You killed someone? Who? Patrick?" My mind spirals and my stomach turns upside down.

"No, that dirty thief knows better than to show up here." My heart sinks as I realize he's talking about Parker. They killed Parker.

"You didn't have to kill him. He was just trying to help," I cry.

"He did help. We never would have found Entael without him," Luca comments.

"What do you want with me?" I ask my hands shaking. "Gavin took the scroll."

"Yes, he did. It turns out that was a very important page indeed. Patrick Flynn was a fool to think he could keep it from us."

"You have the scroll. What more do you want?"

His smile breaks into a vigorous laugh. "More? There is always more isn't there," he says quietly, putting the helmet on the desk. "Complacency is man's greatest mistake." I stare up at him, contemplating the way his nose and mouth resemble his son's. "I see you have activated the perception control device. I'm glad to see it come into use. Tell me, what does it feel like?"

"Why don't you try it out for yourself?" I ask.

"Perhaps some other time, I'm afraid there are other things I want to try." He tilts my jaw up to examine my face, as if it were a book he was trying to decide whether or not to read. I pull away and stare blankly at the black carpet beneath his feet. "Gavin didn't tell me you were so beautiful. It's funny how he hides things, that boy."

"So that's why I'm here. Gavin told you about me. What did he say?"

"He didn't say anything. I knew instantly that he had met someone with an extraordinary gift – the power to slow time. This is very rare indeed," he says taking a cigar from his breast pocket. The flame dancing on the metal lighter reminds me of Gavin. Was he here? Rings of smoke drift through the air like sailboats in the ocean. I can feel the anger rising in my chest.

"Where is Gavin? Does he know I'm here?"

"Yes, he knows. You will see him soon enough – I have plans for the two of you. But first you are going to show me what you can do." I can feel my thoughts spinning out of control and I move uncomfortably in the chair.

"Look, this is not something you want to mess with. I'm not going to perform for you like this is some kind of circus."

"Of course you aren't," he says moving to push a button on the side of the wall. The curtains open to reveal the sun setting on a horizon of treetops. "Antonio!" he calls. A stocky man wearing a brown suit walks swiftly into the room.

"Yes sir?" he asks taking a brief look at me.

"Bring me Eliza."

"Right away sir," Antonio turns on his heel and quickly leaves the room.

"Gavin may have shared with you certain ... talents. We both have the power to transfer life energy. We have passed this ability down four generations. You may find it remarkable how one can extend their own life in this way," he says smashing the smoke of the cigar into a glass ashtray on the desk.

I hear the sound of more footsteps. Antonio enters the room with a short blonde woman walking carefully behind him. She is wearing an old school maid's uniform with a white apron covering a black dress. Her brown eyes stare mainly at the floor and glance furtively over to me.

"Thank you Antonio," Luca says motioning him to go.

"You needed me sir?" Eliza asks uneasily.

"Yes, I require your service in a little experiment." Eliza's eyes widen in fear and I feel my own heart skip a beat as Luca moves behind her and settles his hands around her forehead. A look of panic spreads quickly across her face.

"No, please sir..." Her words stop short as her eyes close and she falls to the floor. Luca's eyes open with a manic stare. He approaches me and I shudder in fear as he moves his hands toward my neck. He looks taller somehow, and his voice almost echoes throughout the room.

"I can feel her life running through my veins," he says. "I hope, for her sake, you can reverse this unfortunate course of events."

His fingers push on a clasp at the back of the metal ring around my neck. It pops open and I breathe a sigh of relief to have it taken off. He withdraws a key from his pocket and inserts it into the handcuffs releasing my arms from the chair. I feel like a glass of water spilling onto the floor as I rush to Eliza's side and find her face still warm. I hold her hand and feel it slowly growing cold. I notice the curve of her lips and feel time slow as I become aware of every particle in her body. Something above us distracts me and I sense it is her – somehow she is watching me hold her body lying lifeless on the floor. She seems so peaceful watching us. I look over to see the sun shimmer its last rays through the trees below. Thousands of glistening lights reflect in my eyes and I realize for the first time there is no reason to fear death. Then, just as clearly as I felt her presence, I sense it disappearing, dissipating into the air. She is gone. I failed her. I look over in disgust at Luca who seems so pleased with himself.

"You k—killed her," I stutter.

"One could say that. Or one might say it was you who failed to bring her back. Cause and effect is ... tricky."

I sob into the flesh of my arm and squeeze the words out. "But you can bring her back."

"Now, now," he consoles. "That won't be necessary. She served a valuable purpose to a most notable cause."

I sit up, enraged. "You're a monster!" I scream. Tears fill my eyes making it impossible to see.

"I've certainly been called much worse," he comments. "The upside is I did notice a change in the quality of the time passing and something else quite surprising..." he says eyeing his palms. He glances at me and I see him push a second button on the wall through the blur of tears.

Within seconds two men bound into the room like wild dogs. They take my arms and pull me back onto the chair. The anger stings in the back of my throat and I glare up at Luca's cold blue eyes as one of the men reattaches the ring around my neck. They carry Eliza's dead body out of the room as if they were emptying the trash.

"They were wrong about you. I don't think you are ever going to see the light," I say in disgust. He turns his head in amusement.

"You're right. I have no interest in "seeing the light" as you say. It is a path for fools." His eyes turn cold again, the smile gone from his face. "I think you have a special gift. Tomorrow we will run some trials," he says flatly.

"You want me to help you? Do you know what I think? I think you can take your trials all the way back to the forgotten little pile evil you came from." His face grimaces as he pretends to be offended. He leans over, his eyes inches away from me. I can smell the cigar smoke on his breath.

"Is that any way to talk to your host?" he whispers. I hold my breath and turn to look out the window. The sun has now completely set and the room is covered by shadow.

"Antonio!" he shouts. The door opens and Antonio enters the room.

"Yes sir?"

"Please see to her needs for this evening. She is to remain bound and under no circumstances is she to remove the, uh, necklace," Luca commands.

"Yes sir," Antonio replies glancing over to inspect the metal cuffs at my hands and the metal "necklace" around my neck.

"This is so wrong," I scold them both. Antonio avoids my gaze while Luca stares back vacantly.

"I hope you have a pleasant evening," Luca comments before closing the door behind him, leaving Antonio standing alone in the room.

"Is there anything I can bring for you?" he asks as if I'm an actual guest at some nice hotel. I continue to stare in silence at the darkened window. He looks confused and hesitates before turning to go. "If there is anything you need, just call for me. I'll be attending the room next door," he says politely, disappearing behind the door.

After I hear the door close, I start to cry. That poor woman, Eliza, she died because of me. I could have just shown him. He didn't have to kill her. And Parker, they killed Parker. I let the tears come and I openly sob alone in the middle of the darkened room. Inhaling spurts and coughs of rage and sadness, the tears eventually draw blanks and I am left with dry, empty sorrow. I wipe my face on my shoulder, trying to clear my head. I can't let this happen to anyone else because of me. I have to get out of here.

I close my eyes and think about Patrick. I remember the mischief of his smile and the flecks of grey in his emerald-green eyes. The smell of cedar fills the room and an image of six intersecting lines above a small circle enters my mind. I sense the words "Don't worry. I'm coming for you."

It's Patrick. I smile at the hint of his presence and feel a guilty pang of relief knowing he's still alive – that it wasn't him.

My mind wanders between possibilities. Should I wait for him? No, he shouldn't even come here. It's too dangerous. I can't let anyone else die because of me, which means I need to get out of here on my own. I take a deep breath and grasp the curving wood of the chair. I gaze openly at the darkness surrounding me. Even in the dark, I can feel the connection forming, the room becoming lighter, the molecules slowing down. I simultaneously feel electric signals pulse out of the metal ring on my spine; a grey cloud permeates my vision and the sound of a high pitch alarm rings in my ear. I breathe deeper, feeling the pulse drift through my spine. I direct it out of the center of my back and feel the cloud lift and the sound fade. I try to focus on my handcuffs. I can feel the weight of them elevating, becoming less dense. I can see tiny metal teeth unclenching and the pins turning simultaneously out to release the locks. I quickly release my arms, undo the clasp on the metal ring binding my neck and breathe a sigh of relief. I am free.

I can still feel the lightness in the room and sense some movement from behind the door. I rush to open it and pause to confirm my suspicions, it is Luca. His dark hair in sharp contrast to the piercing blue of his eyes, he stares resolutely forward, but I see his eyes slowly shifting, taking in my image. Time is speeding up and I quickly move past him down the hall. He turns slowly and I'm shocked to see tiny bolts of electricity flowing haphazardly from his arms. The rays appear randomly and flash in and out of time, illuminating the dark hallway.

"Not ... so ... fast," he says in slow motion.

An adjacent door opens and a figure with dark hair enters the hallway. It's Gavin. His amber eyes look helpless and confused. It's so strange to see him here. My attention shifts, and time fully collides back into the space. I see a flash of lightning hit the wall before it crashes through my shoulder. Blinding pain is the last thing I feel before a veil of pure black envelopes my perception.

Chapter 17

I am back in the mahogany chair, my hands resting on its curved arms. The room is dark and shadows lurk across the floor. Someone is lying face down on the carpet, but I can't see who. Everything seems hazy and I can't make my eyes focus clearly. I struggle to move my legs and kneel down next to the body on the floor. The body seems lifeless and has the shape of a woman. I reach for the person's shoulder and pull as hard as I can. It is as if my arms are too weak to move anything. I lie down on the other side of the body and squint into the darkness, trying to make out the faint impression of a face which slowly fades into a lush cover of grass.

I look up and realize I'm sprawled onto a forest floor. The earth feels cold and wet.

Across a stretch of green grass, I see Patrick. He is reaching to climb a tall willow tree. I see his legs disappear into the canopy as I run to catch him. The trunk of the tree is covered in thick pieces of bark that are easy to grasp and I quickly hoist myself up and reach for the first extending limb. I glimpse Patrick's face. His mischievous grin looks twisted, and the usual light in his green eyes appears wild and unrecognizable. He disappears into the thick shroud of green leaves dancing in the breeze. I climb to where I saw him move and look for any sign of him. I notice a string of leaves slide across my arm. Another string wraps itself around my leg and yet another is yanking on my bag, attempting to steal my things. The tendrils coil around my chest and begin to squeeze the air out of my lungs. I call for help and hear the sound of Patrick's laughter echo in the distance. Suddenly, the branches release me and I am tossed to the ground, fluttering through the air like a falling leaf.

Just before I hit the ground, I am cradled by an elastic net and look up to see Gavin. His smile is warm and his amber eyes are clear. We walk and laugh together through the forest and come to a stretch of blackened earth covered in ash. The landscape has been ravaged by a fire. I look over to see Gavin unconcerned. He motions for me to look again. I observe the darkened forest floor to see tiny sprouts of plants curling up and out of the ground, bright green and glowing with light. Time seems to speed up as I watch life reclaim the space. Within seconds, the forest is restored. Insects and birds fill the air and the sunlight streams though the thick undergrowth enfolding majestic aspen and pine trees. I turn to see Gavin look expectantly into my eyes. His hands reach behind by back and pull me toward him. I release my lips to kiss him and feel heat radiate from his palms. Something inside resists like the turning of a fork in wet sand and my body is wrenched awake, gasping for air.

The morning sunlight blinks its way through thick brown curtains and I feel aching pain from the handcuff digging into my right wrist, binding it to a tall spindle of wood. I look around to find myself in a small bedroom. An antique rocking chair sits in the corner and the ceiling is taller than a normal room. The sheets smell stale, as if they have never been slept in, and I roll onto my back, letting my consciousness return. It was just a dream. Of course it was. Patrick would never act like that. None of it was even possible. I touch my lips, taking comfort in the fact that they never kissed Gavin's willingly. It was just a wild and crazy dream. But this – being kidnapped and kept here, this was not a dream. I let out a quiet laugh full of remorse as I think of how normal my craziest dreams seem compared to my reality lately. I wince at a sharp pain in my left shoulder, and look nervously down to see a dark red burn winding its way down my left arm, spreading across my bicep like the branches of a tree. Images of lightening crashing against the wall flash through my mind. Luca did this. Tears stream down my cheeks and roll past my ears to finally drop onto the dusty pillow below as I comprehend this happened because of me. When I slow time, it makes it possible for Gavin to light fire; Luca must have a similar reaction except he channels electricity. My breath stops short halfway out my lungs as I realize I'm trapped. If I slow time to escape, their power increases.

I am startled by the sound of the door opening. Antonio enters the room carrying a silver tray filled with what looks like a small tea set.

"Would you care for some tea?" he asks. "Breakfast isn't for another half hour, and I thought you would like tea beforehand.

"I'm not hungry," I say trying to comprehend in what world it makes sense to bring me tea when I could definitely use a trip to the doctor. Antonio continues to make tea, pouring the hot water into a tiny cup on the tray. He manages to avoid looking at me, lying handcuffed to the bedpost, with a painful burn sprawled across my shoulder and a trail of tears spread across my face.

"Dr. Fieri insists that you join him," Antonio replies patiently. He leaves the room and returns with a short, dark haired woman wearing a maid's uniform. Instantly, I'm reminded of Eliza and my heartbeat lurches out of my chest. I swallow and try not to let any more tears make their way out of my eyes. "This is Ms. Scott. She will help you dress for the day," Antonio smiles at the floor and quickly turns to leave.

"My name's Maryanne," she explains setting a folded towel and an armful of clothes onto the bed. She looks sympathetically at me, glancing between my right arm hanging from the bedpost and the inflamed burn on my left shoulder. "I think there's some antiseptic in the kitchen. You're going to need to cover that wound."

"Yes please," I say gratefully.

"Dr. Fieri has instructed that I remove the handcuffs for breakfast," she says cheerfully. I breathe a long sigh of relief which is curtailed as her eyes become serious. "He also ordered some men to wait outside the room to escort you." She turns a small key into the lock and I clutch my arm to my chest, feeling the blood re-circulate through it.

"The bathroom is through here," she opens a door next to the bed. "I think you'll find everything you need. I'll be back with the antiseptic and some bandages."

"Thank you," I manage.

The bathroom is covered in cold white tile and I stumble across it to find my reflection in the mirror. My eyes are raw from crying and filled with a desperation I've never seen in them before. I splash some cold water on my face and try to regain some part of the Amy I'm used to seeing. I run my fingers across my face, wiping away the excess water, and blinking my wet eyelashes slowly, I stare openly into their reflection. I feel my heart beating oxygen throughout my body and exhale every last particle of air out of my lungs. In this moment my reflection in the mirror is blurred but I see myself more clearly. I am alive. I feel energy penetrate the air around me in a constant stream from my heart through my feet. A twinge of desire oscillates in my chest at the memory of being trapped, and I focus my attention there, at the center of the desire, shifting it into an image of my freedom. I will be free. I can see it.

Slowly the realization fades and I see my face staring back in the mirror. I take my shirt off and gasp at the blackened patch of skin where the electric bolt hit my shoulder. The pain makes it hard to breathe and I carefully turn the faucet in the shower, letting steam fill the room. I step gingerly into the shower and turn to let the hot blanket of water cover my back. Occasionally a stream of water shoots down my shoulder sending a burning trail of heat down my arm. My thoughts turn to Gavin, and I see him running toward me down the hallway, his hands reaching out to catch me. I smile fondly at the memory of him as I wash the soap out of my hair. His amber eyes shining in the darkness, like a panther. I think he truly cares for me. Maybe I would be better off with him; we could start a new life somewhere and be completely free.

The wave of fantasy is cut short and I get a strange feeling. I suddenly feel incredibly vulnerable, as if someone else is in the shower with me, and I instinctively cover my chest, glancing carefully behind me. There's nothing there, and I realize the entity isn't physical. It's in my head. Gavin is controlling my thoughts. He must be. He has the remaining page of Indus script, and with it he can implant whatever thoughts he wants. I slam the water off and rip open the shower curtain. My anger outweighs my fear and I storm out of the shower and throw a towel aimlessly around my chest. He's the reason for the dreams I had. It was him trying to make me forget about Eliza. It was him making Patrick abandon me. It was all him.

I glance frantically around the bathroom and see a picture of a hunting scene. Men on horses drawn with white pants and black hats lead by a pack of dogs, presumably to chase a poor defenseless animal across the river. Enraged, I take the picture and smash it across the sink, and let out a scream of insanity. Breathing heavily from destroying the glass frame, I carefully step over the shards of glass, and reposition my towel, feeling emboldened. I open the bathroom door to see Maryanne looking shocked.

"Is everything okay?" she asks hesitantly. I shake my head in exasperation.

"They are serving breakfast in the dining hall. We should get you ready," she says swiftly.

"Yes. Let's go to breakfast," I fume. At this moment, my desire to rip Gavin's head off outweighs my fear of his father, or even my need to escape.

Maryanne sits me down on the bed and pulls my hair off of my left shoulder. I can tell by the look on her face it's as bad as I thought, and I hold my breath as she dabs a cotton ball soaked in alcohol across the charred black skin on my shoulder. She covers it with gauze; the scarlet branches from the burn jetting out from below the bandage.

"Thank you," I say. Her eyes light up and I notice she's strikingly beautiful. The color of her skin reminds me of my mother, and I recognize the shape of the white hat covering her dark hair. "You knew Eliza?" I ask. She nods her head and tears run effortlessly down her cheeks.

"She was my friend," she cries.

"I'm so sorry," I say hugging her. "You really should get of here. You shouldn't work for these people."

"I can't," she sobs. "They will kill me if I leave. You don't understand."

I hug her closer, and try to think of a way to make it all better. She pulls back, shakes her head and tries to smile.

"I don't know what I was thinking. Please forgive me," she says. I wipe a tear from her cheek and stare deeply into her helpless eyes.

"I'm leaving soon. You should come," I say. She laughs and shakes her head in disbelief.

"I have to get you ready for breakfast," she says holding up a white silk dress.

"I'm not staying that long," I explain lowering the silken garment. She raises her eyebrow as I return to the bathroom and put on my dirty jeans and t-shirt.

"I'm serious. I will leave this place, and you should come with me," I say shutting off the bathroom light.

"That's impossible," she says. The sweetness in her eyes drops as she looks at the floor and swings open the bedroom door to reveal four men facing the doorway, waiting for me.

I just stand there, looking at them in disbelief. One of the men steps back and motions for me to walk down the hall. The other three stare at me with unflinching eyes, not trusting my hesitation. "I'm coming," I manage. I force myself to step into the hall taking one last look at Maryanne's beautiful face staring motionless at the floor.

With two men walking in front and two behind, we make our way down three flights of stairs. I remember how Patrick talked about them, as if they were little babies or hamsters, totally harmless. I smile at the thought of him, and run my fingers down the staircase railing, feeling the carved creviced lining run under my fingers. I can sense the rhythm of the men's footsteps and imagine the one in front tripping down the stairs. Although he doesn't completely fall, I notice his foot stumble, and he reaches for the railing to hold himself up. At the bottom of the stairs we round the corner to see a wide dining hall filled with light streaming through tall stained glass windows. A white linen cloth spreads across a long table which runs nearly the length of the room and is covered in bowls of fruit and silver trays. Gavin and Luca are sitting at the end of the table.

"So nice to see you could join us," Luca calls motioning with his knife for me to sit down next to him.

The forced kindness in his voice sends a shiver down my spine as I walk the length of the room followed by all four men. Luca nods for them to stand back as I pull out the heavy wooden chair to sit down next to him. Gavin sits directly across from me. Wearing his usual black leather jacket, he idly plays with a silver fork, rolling it back and forth on the table.

"We have a big day today," Luca says, his eyes growing wider. "Lots of ... fun. Gavin is convinced the perception control device is unnecessary." Gavin glances at me expectantly. "I hope for your sake he's right." Luca cuts into a large chunk of red meat and plunges a piece into his mouth, chewing profusely.

I watch Gavin's face as he stares back at the flashing silver slipping between his fingers. My anger rising, I focus my thoughts toward him. "I can't believe you let them kill Parker. He was your friend. You can't change my mind. I'll never be with you," I think staring at him. His eyes rise to meet mine and I see a hint of sadness spread across his face which he quickly hides by resuming his contemplation of his silverware.

"Our family has been channeling energy for generations, with ... much success. But I've never experienced the intensity of power I enjoyed last night. So much force, and it came with such ease," Luca comments casually while sawing into another cut of red meat. "I think we are just skimming the surface here. After breakfast we will convene in the cellar. I want to measure the true extent of this ... influence."

"And what if I refuse?" I ask shaking inside.

"We have our methods of persuasion, don't we Gavin?"

"Yes father," Gavin answers reluctantly. His eyes remain fixated on the table.

"To avoid the inconvenience of ambiguity, let me be as precise as possible," Luca says laying down his fork and touching the stained edge of his knife. "If you refuse, then we will kill you," he says slicing the blade through the air to rest heavily against my throat. I brace myself against the back of the chair and look to see Gavin is distracted by something across the room.

"Last time I checked, that's not where we place our cutlery when we are done eating." A voice calls out from the corner of the room. It's Patrick. He's here.

Chapter 18

I glance over to see Patrick leaning against the staircase, eyeing us all casually. Luca takes the knife from my throat and sends it flying through the air toward Patrick's head. Patrick leans slightly to the left and the knife slams with a dull thud into the wall behind him.

"Seize him!" Luca shouts at the men lining the wall.

All four of the men are already lunging toward Patrick. Patrick is grinning like a five year old and strikes his best karate pose before he rolls under the first two men attempting to tackle him. The men run into each other and fall like bowling pins.

"Suckers!" I hear Patrick shout.

Luca's arm reaches around my neck and he pulls me up, trying to drag me out of the room. I shriek from the pain shooting out of my shoulder and watch as Patrick dodges a second attack. He pulls on the white sheet on the table sending food and silver plates flying in the air. I watch in slow motion as a white porcelain saucer spins up into the air and feel goose bumps run down my arms. The room feels lighter, and time slows enough for me to pull Luca's arm off of my neck and knee him forcefully in the groin. Luca kneels down in slow motion. My self-defense teacher wasn't kidding around when he emphasized that move.

Patrick jumps up onto the table and swings from the chandelier in slow motion kicking Gavin's face. I watch in horror as the table lights on fire. Gavin's eyes are lit up and he flings balls of fire at Patrick as he jumps off of the burning surface and lands by my side. I grasp his hand and feel his pulse beating hard against my palm, our hearts linking. Waves of energy circulate between us, and our thoughts align and focus on the same course. In one sweeping motion we send the giant wooden block of a table hurling toward Gavin and Luca, trapping them in a cage of flame.

Luca's arms spontaneously erupt with cracks of electricity, and we run toward the back door narrowly missing the bolt that crashes into the stained glass window behind us. Time moves in spurts, and I feel Patrick pull me back. He redirects a fire ball and motions for the floor boards to lift up throwing both Gavin and Luca off their feet. We run out of the back kitchen door sending two bags of rice shooting like bullets behind us.

The backyard is covered in thick green grass that extends in waves undulating down and ending in a thick forest. I find myself pulling Patrick's arm to get him to move faster down the countless grassy hills. Bolts of lightning crash all around us and I turn to see Luca chasing us, followed by Gavin. We duck under one of the hills, and Patrick motions for a pile of rocks to rise and sends them flying at Luca and Gavin. They dodge the swarm of rocks hurling toward them, as I watch in slow motion. A bolt of electricity flies out of Luca's hand, lumbering haphazardly toward Patrick. I push him down the hill, clearing the path and feel the lightning crack against my chest. The bolt sends pain running throughout my entire body, shocks my nervous system, and flings me onto the ground. A second bolt shoots across the grass and I close my eyes, unable to move, bracing myself against the searing pain I know will come. At the last second, I open my eyes to see Gavin, sprinting in front of me, deflect the bolt of electricity. He rolls across the grass, writhing in pain.

I pull myself over to him and take his head in my hands. As he closes his eyes I sense the words, "I love you," and he manages a weak smile before he loses consciousness. Shaking, I reach down and feel for his wrist, desperately hoping to find a pulse. There isn't one. Gavin is gone. I look up to see Luca and Patrick walking toward us. Luca's skin is the color of grey sky as he falls to the ground at Gavin's side.

"Can you bring him back?" I ask hopefully. Luca reaches down and places his hands on Gavin's temples. Moments pass and nothing happens. Panic starts to set in and I realize there is no other way. I have to try to reverse time. I reach over and touch Luca's arm as he rocks back and forth in a frenzy holding his son. "You have to trust me," I say quietly. I run my hand along the black studded leather of Gavin's jacket, and observe the shape of his nose angling down, a larger version of his childhood face. The air begins to pulse and time begins to slow. I hear Patrick's voice echo through the warm air.

"No, Amy. Please don't. It's not worth the risk," he pleads falling to my side.

"I have to try," I reply looking at least one last time into his clear green eyes filling with tears.

The earth hums under my feet and I can see the blades of grass shifting in and out of the light. I feel my own cells spinning to become weightless. Everything seems to float in the air and form becomes light. I can no longer see myself, and instead I am drifting in and out of everything. It is all connected, and every possibility exists in a state of pure potential. I slowly realign the formless energy, imagining Gavin standing behind Luca. The second bolt of lightning is wiped from existence just as I feel myself fading. Time speeds up, leaving me lost in between.

I look at Luca's face as he is just about to shoot the second bolt. Gavin moves from behind him, coming to protect me, but this time Luca lowers his arms and looks at Gavin. Somehow, he knows.

"Amy!" Patrick screams. "Amy, where are you?" He screams, frantically searching the ground with his hands, unable to see me.

"I'm right here!" I call. No one hears me. I can barely make out the impression of being in my body, and try to remember what it feels like to breathe air. Patrick's hand stumbles over the space where my chest should be and he stops short, recognizing my energy. He rests his hand on my heart and slowly I can feel the pulse forming. I keep breathing in my mind until finally I feel the pull of real air into my lungs. I'm back. I came back. I look up and feel Patrick's lips falling onto my own, his warm breath on my face.

"You're alive!" he cries.

I look happily at my hands, and the existence of all the solid matter around me. I notice white strands of hair lying in the grass.

"What's this?" I ask reaching to touch the strange colored hair at my side. "This is my hair?" I ask in astonishment. My hair came back completely white. I stare in shock for a moment and look disappointedly up at Patrick.

"I'm just so glad you're alive," he cries again. "We need to get you to a hospital." He gingerly picks me up and begins to carry me towards the gated entrance at the front of the house.

I look behind us to see Luca holding Gavin's arm back, letting us go. His cold, calculating, arctic blue eyes flash a hint of gratitude, if only for a moment.

"We can't leave without Maryanne," I say. Just then I see her making her way down the long path of stairs pouring out the front entrance.

"I'm coming with you," she says with a smile, pulling her dark hair out of her maid's headpiece. Her eyes shine with a confidence that makes her beauty radiant in the sunlight. She pushes a button on the tall cast iron gate and it swings open, letting us pass out of sight of the Necoli Castle, hopefully forever.

Chapter 19

After a trip in an ambulance, I find myself lying in a hospital bed drifting in and out of sleep. Patrick holds my hand underneath a heavy traffic of hospital wires. A monitor on my heart beeps steadily, and I watch it attentively, feeling reassured with each passing beep. My doctor is a short blonde woman with a Swedish accent.

"You are going to be alright," she says checking a list on her clipboard. "You were struck by lightning not once, but twice. You are very lucky to be here. The scars should heal in time, and I see no evidence of brain damage. Your heart is doing well. I would like to keep you overnight, and if everything remains unchanged, you can go home tomorrow. There is something ... unexplainable about your hair. I've never seen anything like it before. I don't think it will be changing anytime soon, but it might grow back normal."

I inspect the white strands of hair on my shoulder and wonder if the rest of me will grow back "normal".

When my mom and Ana finally arrive, I almost can't believe it, expecting the door to reveal yet another stream of nurses. I notice Ana has my bag and I eagerly feel the canvas for the familiar shape of my phone.

"Oh, sweetie! Are you okay? What happened? Your hair!" My mom swoops down and her hug lasts long enough for my heartbeat to slow down to "resting". When she finally pulls back I see the extreme worry in her eyes. She looks horrible, and so tired.

"I'm so sorry mom," I say softly.

"Ana has tried to ex - explain," she stutters. "You've been tra - traveling time? Are you okay? Is this true? How did this h – happen?"

"I'm okay, everything is alright. I'll tell you everything," I say. I proceed to tell my mother the events of my week from the second I started lying to her. The nurses come in at the sound of yelling voices when she realizes Patrick's role in what happened and Ana forces him to leave the room with her.

"So you have the ability to slow time?" my mother asks again.

"Pretty much," I confirm. "I know it sounds crazy."

"And you drove to New Mexico with Ana's son – Patrick, and stayed there with her for the week?"

"Yea," I say.

"And then you were kidnapped and brought out here?" she cries. I nod my head and pass her the box of tissues. "And you were struck by lightning?"

"More like electrical bolts coming out of a man's hands, but yea, basically."

"When Ana called me I didn't know what to think. I thought you were at Ally's and it was some kind of a trick. You can't ... you can't lie to me like this ever again."

"I know. I'm so sorry," I say hugging her.

Later, when she is passed out, asleep across my feet, I draw a picture of a dragonfly and tuck it into her pocket. I know it will be a long time before my mom fully trusts me again, and even longer before she understands the full extent of what has happened to me. I am grateful to have the time it takes with her, and I know she will eventually get it, sort of.

After a plane ride and an hour-long drive, I'm home. I can't believe how great it is to see my stuff. I grab my teddy bear, settle into my bed and sleep for eighteen hours straight. It's Sunday evening when I finally wake up. My phone is lit up and there are seven text messages, four from Ally and three from Patrick. After an hour long conversation with Ally, where I convince her that she didn't just ruin my life and that she should definitely come out for the weekend, I call Patrick.

"Amy?" He answers the phone.

"Hey," I say.

"How's it going?" he asks carefully.

"Good, I feel a lot better."

His sigh of relief is palpable. "That's good," he manages.

"So Maryanne went back to Entael with your mom?" I ask.

"Yea, my mom thought that would be best."

"That was a super scary place," I say quietly. There is a long pause on the line and I begin to think he didn't hear me.

Finally, his words burst out in a flurry of remorse. "I'm so sorry. I keep telling myself this is all my fault, and that I should never have asked you to come. Your mom is right to hate my guts."

I pause to let his words sink in, working out the contours of how I feel.

"After everything we've been through, I can't imagine taking it back," I say softly. "I would do it again." There is an even longer pause and I almost wonder if we got disconnected. Then I hear him crying.

"When you didn't come back we looked everywhere. Parker saw you in the Necoli Castle and insisted on going alone. I should have gone with him, but he wouldn't let me. He said it was his responsibility. He should have let me come. I know how to deal with them. I could have saved him," Patrick sobs. I can feel the regret knotting itself up in him, his voice shaking. I grasp the phone tighter, wanting to hold him, to comfort him somehow.

"It's not your fault."

"When we didn't hear from him, Grace tried to channel him and she found out he was gone. He died. They killed him."

"It's not your fault," I say again. "I know this is going to sound weird, but I can feel him. Up there somehow, watching." I listen as he inhales a full breath of air.

"I know what you mean," he says exhaling. "It's like he's still remotely viewing us. He was such a great friend." Then his words pour out like hail in a rainstorm. "I should have gone there with him. When I heard what they did, I was so mad, Amy. The only thing that kept me calm was thinking of you. I should have come sooner. I'm so sorry. I promise I'll take care of the Valencia forever. They will never hurt you again. I promise..."

"Don't say that," I interrupt. "I don't want to mess with them anymore. Let's just leave them alone," I plead. There is another long pause on the line, and I bite my lip, waiting for his response.

"If you say so," he reluctantly replies. "How's your mom?" he asks changing the subject.

"She's still a little shell-shocked, but I think she'll be alright. I can't lie to her anymore. If there's one thing I know right now, it's that I'm done keeping secrets. No more secrets."

"No secrets? Really? Not from anyone?" he asks surprised. "Not about anything?

"Not anything. People have a right to know the truth, and for better or worse, I'm not going to hide it from them." I am a little surprised by the tenacity in my voice.

"Well, this should be interesting," he laughs.

"You think I'm joking," I counter.

"No, I can tell you're serious. It's just that most people aren't ready for this. They either won't believe you or you'll end up in some institution getting prodded with wires if they do."

"I think that some people are ready," I reply.

"Maybe. Maybe some are. Just be careful. It wasn't that long ago that they ran around burning people at the stake you know?"

"I don't think they make stakes anymore. Anyway, I just think there are more of us out there. You know, people who can feel this."

"Sure there are, but there are just as many people who can't. Just be mindful okay?"

"Alright, mom. I'll wear the helmet, and won't talk to strangers," I joke.

"I'm serious."

"Unless they have candy," I laugh.

"Amy."

"Okay! I'll be careful," I promise. "Whatever happened to practicing nonattachment? To letting go?"

"I guess it's not so easy when you care for someone the way I care for you. What can I say? I'm hooked. You reel me in anytime."

"Anytime?" I ask flirtatiously.

"All the time."

I pause and ponder the implications of all the time. "Does this mean we can't be enlightened? What would your gurus say?"

"I don't care what they say. And in any case, I think you've had enough light for one week. Are you going to school tomorrow?

School. After everything I've been through it's hard to imagine wanting to go back there, but a part of me needs something normal, something routine for a change.

"I was planning on it," I say.

"Great. I'll pick you up in 'the Fugitive'."

"So now you want to drive my car?" I ask playfully.

"I have no other car, remember?"

"Right. I'll see you at seven," I say.

"Goodnight Amy," he says softly.

"Goodnight," I whisper pressing the phone off.

The alarm seems to come too early at 6:05 a.m. I roll over to push the snooze button, still in partial denial about school. I hear a knock at my door. It's my mom. She's being extra-overly protective because she feels guilty for almost losing me even though it's not even remotely her fault. Go figure.

"Are you sure you're ready to go back to school today?" she asks peeping her head in.

"Um-hm. Totally," I moan.

"Because I can call in right now and you can just stay home," she offers. I fling the cover off my legs and hurl myself out of bed.

"No mom, it's okay. I'm up," I reply.

Hot shower water runs across my forehead, streaming down my shoulders. The wounds on my chest and shoulder still burn from the heat of the water, but already I can feel a new layer of skin forming. I breathe the warm air, thick with particles of water, and shampoo the fibers of my long white hair. I wonder if maybe I should go have it dyed back to "normal".

I dry my hair carefully with the towel and get dressed. Standing in front of the mirror, I inspect myself. My sky-blue eyes are clear, and resonate with a sad but wise knowledge. Long white strands of hair cascade next to my face, and somehow make my skin look more tan than usual. Maybe having white hair isn't so bad after all. I convince myself the red scar on my shoulder almost looks like a tattoo as I gear up to give myself a pep talk, wondering if I'm going to be able to smile for real this time.

"Okay self. You've been through a lot. Some good and some ... not so good. Your job today is to take the good and rock it. Don't stop. Just keep rocking it, until the bell rings." I pause and wait. After a few moments, I feel a surge of bliss rising in my chest, bursting forth into a full-blown, uncontained smile.

About the Author

Lindsey Madison believes in everyday enlightenment and enjoys writing fiction that explores the boundaries of consciousness. She currently lives in Colorado where she is working on a sequel for her first novel, "Shift".

Connect with me online at https://www.smashwords.com/profile/view/madisondunn

www.ingramcontent.com/pod-product-compliance
Lightning Source LLC
Chambersburg PA
CBHW030240160726
47987CB00020B/477